VERY IRRESISTIBLE PLAYBOY

BILLIONAIRE BACHELORS: BOOK 1

LILA MONROE

LILA MONROE BOOKS

Very Irresistible Playboy
Billionaire Bachelors: Book 1

Welcome to Billionaire Bachelors Inc, where the sexiest men in the city are about to meet their match..

Hot bachelor Max Carlisle is heir to a media empire, tabloid catnip, and... wants to hire me to be his fake fiancee. I know what it takes to keep a billionaire in line, but signing up for seven days in close quarters with this Very Irresistible Playboy? It's just asking for trouble. The kind of thrilling, reckless trouble I could use a little more of since my career is currently ass-backwards in a mud bath with six shih-tzus (don't ask).

So do I:

a) Take the job, and bicker wildly every step of the way?

b) Embark on a mad-cap treasure hunt to claim his billion-dollar inheritance?

c) Try my hardest not to fall head-over-heels in love with him and wind up having the best sex of my life?

d) All of the above?

Something tells me I'm about to be way out of my league... and under the most handsome, infuriating man I've ever met. But with a fortune on the line, can we beat out his crazy relatives to win the prize? And will our fake relationship be game over at the finish line?

Find out in the new sexy, hilarious romantic comedy from Lila Monroe!

Billionaire Bachelors Series:
1. Very Irresistible Playboy
2. Hot Daddy (April)
3. Wild Card (June)
4. Man Candy (Aug)

ALSO BY LILA:

1

HALLIE

THE ONLY THING worse than showing up late for the wedding you're supposed to shoot? Showing up late *and* finding the groom banging a bridesmaid in the bathroom.

I freeze with my hand on the door, not believing what I'm seeing. Mr. Newlywed and Miss Teal Taffeta are so busy going at it they don't even notice me. He's got her up on the sink counter, and if adultery was an Olympic sport, I'd have to give them at least a 6 on the difficulty scale. And with that poofy bridesmaid dress practically swallowing him whole? A solid 7 out of 10, for sure.

Minus 15 for the whole "nasty cheaters" side of things, I mean.

I'm just thinking about sidling on past to reach a stall when his pale ass bobs over the waist of his tuxedo pants. I reel back. Okay, I don't need to pee *that* bad.

I stage a hasty retreat, back into the garlands and glitter strewn around the Central Park Boathouse. Now that's a much prettier view. We're set up by the building, with five crystal-bedecked white tents overlooking the lake. Even the trees are dripping with crystals, along-side bundles of white roses by the dozen, as the wedding guests sit down for their lavish meal. This has to be the most fancypants wedding I've ever been to, but I'm not a guest—I'm on the job today, ready to capture these beautiful memories in pictures that will last a lifetime.

Minus the banging, of course.

I look around for my boss for the day, aka the most in-demand wedding photographer on the East Coast. I've become Frederico's go-to person when his usual assistant decides to play hooky, and despite the fact he's a fiery bundle of Spanish artistic temperament, when he called me up this morning I couldn't afford to turn the gig down. Literally. I just signed over the last of my savings to cover this month's rent check.

Question: Will the happy couple still pay for wedding pictures if they've already broken up before the end of the celebration?

Don't get me wrong. I've got a conscience. I just watched Mr. Newlywed say his vows. Captured photographic evidence of it, too. So with that image from the bathroom burned into my mind, I'm scrambling to think of what to do. Whether I should tell someone. *How* I should tell someone. Is an anonymous note a possibility? Because you know what they say about shooting the messenger and all . . .

I go looking for Frederico to solve this particular moral dilemma, but when I check the nearest storage tent—

Holy hell, there's the bride pressed up against one of the tables, tongue-wrestling some dude with a man bun.

I pause in shock, but there's no mistaking her. I mean, the big white dress is a pretty major giveaway. The big white dress she's letting Man Bun push his hands up under, all the way to her—

Yup. Something blue.

What's *with* these people?

You know what? I don't want to know. Maybe they have the openest of open relationships. Maybe two really scummy people just got hitched. Either way, it's none of my business. They seem happy enough . . . completely separate from each other. Who am I to interfere?

Or get in the way of my paycheck.

I backtrack, straight into a puddle of mud. Ugh. I pry my sling-backs out with a sigh.

Somehow, I thought being a pro photographer was going to be a lot more glamorous than this. I guess that's what I get for putting my career dreams on hold. I'd been working as an executive assistant for a few years; I always told myself it was temporary, but one day, I took a look around and realized my dreams weren't any closer than when I graduated. I took the plunge, quit my day job . . . and now I'm stuck at the bottom of the ladder starting over again. One rung at a time.

But there are some benefits along the way. My gaze falls on the catering tent, and my stomach lets out an almighty rumble. I skipped lunch shooting the bridal party prep, and everyone is busy right now stuffing their faces under the main awning. Since nobody wants photographs of themselves with a mouthful of steak, maybe this is the perfect moment to sneak a tasty little snack.

I slink over and peek past the draped lengths of sparkly gauze. The servers are still whisking out the hot food, but there's a big spread of drool-worthy desserts just waiting on one of the tables. My stomach gets louder. I slip past the gauze and snag a chocolate cupcake.

The buttercream icing melts in my mouth. Fuck, that is a perfect mouth-gasm right there. I gulp it down and look at the table again. The lemon ones look irresistible too.

You're never supposed to eat just *one* cupcake, right?

I'm just raising my second illicit treat to my lips when a man ducks into the tent. "Busted!"

I freeze. The guy laughs. "Sorry, you just looked so guilty. Mmm, chocolate . . ." He strolls over, grabs a cake, and shoots me a smile so warm I'm surprised the icing doesn't melt in my hand.

Speaking of drool-worthy? Exhibit A is right in front of me. With that tawny hair and the sexy hint of scruff on his square jaw, he looks like Chris Pine in that tux, only twice as hot.

Where the hell did he come from, and can I get a first-class ticket there?

"Relax," he says, with a low rich voice that could melt all sorts of other things. "I won't tell if you don't." He winks and licks the frosting right off the top in a way that should be illegal. "So, who are you hiding from?"

"I'm not hiding," I protest. "Well, maybe just a little. I'm supposed to be shooting the happy couple, but—" I stop myself, realizing just in time that I was planning to be discreet.

But Mr. Hunky Pants is clearly in on the secret, because he gives me a sympathetic grin. "But they're off busy with their *friends*?"

"You know about that?" I ask, relieved. "What's their deal?"

"Hey, it takes all kinds." He shrugs, devouring another dessert. "I heard that sometimes they even share."

I choke on my cupcake. He laughs, and passes me a glass of champagne. I gulp it down, my eyes streaming. "You know what? I don't even want to know. I was never here."

"Excellent strategy," he agrees. "Just as long as you promise not to tell the bride's mother you saw me."

It's my turn to arch an eyebrow. "Have you been getting into trouble?"

"Not exactly. More trying to stay out of it. Mrs. Collingwood is very determined to set me up with a date. Which I wouldn't necessarily have a problem with, except she seems to be aiming to set me up with *her*." He makes a face.

I have to laugh. "Oh, poor you," I tease. "So many women throwing themselves at you, you have to run and hide."

"Hey," he protests, grinning. "I enjoy women throwing themselves at me, if they're the right women." He gives me a quick once-over. "You, for example, are welcome to give it a try."

"Tempting." I keep my tone light, even as the devil on my shoulder swoons. "But I'm here for business, not pleasure."

"Personally, I don't see anything wrong with mixing the two." He keeps smiling. "It always works out just fine for me."

Sure it does. But I used to work for the wealthiest playboy in the city, and I know the downside to guys like this. They're all flash and dazzle: whisking you off to luxurious resorts and wining and dining you . . . before losing interest, moving onto the next shiny toy, and breaking your heart.

Cynical? Me? I prefer to think of it as keeping one foot firmly on the ground. It was my (unofficial) job to break the news to the discarded girlfriends after my boss decided to move along. And sure, he shaped up in the end after he fell in love, but watching him act like, well, a total manwhore for years made me wise to the playboy *modus operandi*. I've sworn to steer clear of men with more charm than substance.

Like this Hottie McHotterson right here in front of me.

"I'm Max, by the way," he says, offering the hand that's not occupied with a cupcake.

I take it, ignoring the heat from his firm grip. "Hallie. Assistant photographer for the day."

"What a day, isn't it? I thought the priest was going to have a nervous breakdown by the time the flower girl made it down the aisle."

"That's nothing," I tell him ruefully. "The wedding I shot last month, the guy officiating answered his own call for objections, got down on bended knee, and asked the bride if she'd marry him instead."

Max snorts and nearly chokes on his cupcake, which somehow makes him even more attractive. "You're joking."

"Nuh-uh. The worst part—or best, if we're going for entertainment value—is she actually seemed to consider it before she turned him down. And then they still let him do the ceremony!" I exclaim. "If I were wagering, I'd give that couple three months, tops."

"Okay," Max says, "but I bet you've never been to a wedding where the father of the bride got so drunk during the reception he stripped naked and dove into the wedding cake."

This time, both my eyebrows shoot up. "What kind of company do you keep, exactly?"

"Oh, you know, a little of this, a little of that. I get around." His smile turns slightly wolfish.

"I bet you do." I give him a look, but he just laughs.

"So, what do you say we blow this joint?" he asks. "Go have ourselves some fun."

"Didn't you hear the part where I said I'm working?" I ask, amazed at his confidence. "I can't just bail."

"Why not?"

I roll my eyes. Of course, a man in a designer tux and ten-thousand-dollar watch wouldn't care about a little thing like a paycheck.

"Oh, come on." Max leans closer, and the heat of his body washes over me. I swear I feel my panties dampening just like that. "Live a little."

I pause. It's been too long since I did something crazy, and he is the hottest thing I've seen in, well, *ever* . . .

Do it, my devil whispers, despite all my pledges to be sensible. *Do it twice, and then again in the morning.*

I open my mouth to reply, but suddenly, a shrill voice carries from beyond the tent.

"Max? Oh Maxie-boy!"

Max stiffens. "Damn," he mutters under his breath. "She's found me."

"Persistent, is she?" I murmur, stifling a giggle. "You'd almost think you were a real catch or something."

Footsteps rustle. A sinewy hand pushes the sparkly gauze aside. I catch a glimpse of a gaunt, haughty face topped by an updo that would make Marge Simpson proud, and then Max is cupping my jaw, pulling my face to his.

He kisses me like it's the most natural thing in the world. Hot and slow, his mouth seductively easing my lips open. *Hello*. A shiver of pleasure races through me as he angles his head to deepen the kiss. His arm wraps around my waist and pulls me right up against his solid body. Yep, he's all muscle under that suit. Muscles I suddenly find myself really, really wanting to run my hands all over. For research's sake, obviously.

There's a huff from Mrs. Collingwood, and then she's stalking away. I'm too busy seeing stars to care. Then Max lets me go, and I realize we're alone again. He grins at me, a spark dancing in his blue-gray eyes.

"There," he grins. "That should throw her off the scent. Well, I won't keep you any longer. Thanks for the help."

He gives me a quick salute, then saunters out of the tent as if nothing all that important just happened.

Oh my God.

I sink back against the nearest chair, still reeling from that incredible kiss. I wasn't even sure about having a drink with him, and now I'm disappointed he didn't stick around to ravish me on the cupcake table.

Where's a cold shower when you need one? Apparently the whole "getting it on with anyone, anywhere" atmosphere has infected the entire guest list, including me.

But I'm not really a guest. As becomes even more obvious a second later with the boom of Frederico's voice.

"Hallie! I need you over by the lake, stat!"

The last effects of the kiss evaporate. I grab my camera and scamper out of the tent.

Frederico strides over to meet me. Somehow he manages to look manic and stern at the same time. "The dogs," he says, pointing vaguely behind him. "And then I need you inside."

He starts to walk off as if he's given me any actual instructions. "Um, what about the dogs?"

"The canine 'bridal party' is waiting for their photographs down by the lake. I think they're getting a little impatient."

Bridal dogs. OK.

I hurry towards the lake, where some poor assistant is clutching the leashes of six yappy shih-tzus. And they each have a white collar fixed around their necks glittering with what look like real diamonds.

Of course they're accessorized better than me.

"Lucky and Pebbles are Trista's," the assistant babbles as I pull out my camera. "She wants lots of pictures of them especially. And you can get some groupings by family, right? Chance is her parents' dog. And of course we have to get them all together."

"No problem!" I manage to hold my amusement in check and get to work. The light is pretty good here, the afternoon sun beaming over the lawn between the trees. But the click of the camera seems to stir up the dogs.

"Hey, hey," the assistant says nervously, as they tug at their leashes. "Settle down!"

"Just keep them together for one group shot!" I call encouragingly. I back up towards the dock, trying to get them centered in the frame. "One more minute, I promise!"

Suddenly, a yappy fight breaks out, and one of them lunges— breaking free. "Come back! Lucky! Stay!" The assistant is powerless, and the next thing I know, all six of the furry wedding guests are charging straight at me.

I yelp, scooting to the side. Two of them veer to cut me off while the others race toward me from the other side. "Good doggies, good doggies!" I plead, dodging their eager paws. Their leashes whip around my ankles, and before I can free myself, one leaps right at my legs. I stumble backwards, and lose my footing on the dock.

SPLASH.

I tumble backwards into the cold lake.

Move over, ladies and gentlemen—"worst wedding ever" has a new winner.

2

HALLIE

"STILL GRIEVING YOUR CAMERA?" my roommate Jules asks as she breezes through the living room the next morning. She grabs her toast just as it pops out of the toaster and takes a bite in the same motion. Jules is a master of efficiency. She has to be, or the law firm she's trying to make partner at would already have worked her into an early grave.

I set my poor, waterlogged hunk of equipment down and sigh. "It's not a camera anymore. A camera is something you can take pictures with. *That* is a very expensive paperweight."

Unfortunately, when I crashed into the lake yesterday, my baby crashed with me, and no amount of coaxing, begging, pleading, and crying has convinced it to turn on since then.

What do you call a photographer without a proper camera?

Broke. And also, screwed. If it wasn't for the truly excellent kiss I got out of the event, the whole day would go down in history as one of my least shining moments ever.

Jules pauses by the back of the couch to assess the situation. With her power-suit getup and her black hair pulled back into a smooth French twist, she looks every inch the corporate badass lawyer.

"Won't your insurance cover it?"

"Is there anything insurance actually covers?" I ask, then sigh. "I already checked. No can do."

"Well, that's ridiculous. How about I write them a super-threatening lawyer letter to tell them to smarten up?"

I perk up. "Do you really think that would work?"

She gives me a sympathetic smile. "No. But it might be satisfying anyway."

I wave her off. "Never mind then. I don't want you damaging your professional cred. I just need to get a job, and then I can buy a new camera. Of course, to get a photography job, I need actual photography equipment . . ." I trail off, wincing at my catch-22. "Don't worry, I'll figure something out. I always do."

"That's the spirit," Jules says.

"And I've got an interview today," I add.

"See?" Jules declares. "This is just a hiccup. Is the job anywhere good?"

"Carlisle Publishing," I answer, feeling a spark of excitement. "Junior staff photographer for one of their life and culture magazines. It would be amazing: I could build up my portfolio, get tons of experience, and learn from some of their big hitters . . ."

"After they see your pictures, they'd be idiots not to take you on." Jules gives my arm a reassuring squeeze and looks at her watch at the same time. "Crap. I've got to jet, or I'll miss that eight o'clock meeting. Good luck with the interview!"

I CHANGE into my best "hire me" outfit (minimal wrinkles, maximum Girl Friday vibes) and head uptown on the subway with plenty of time to spare. After spending years as a personal assistant to a demanding investment genius, I'm used to thinking of all the tiny details. So, I plan a backup train route in case there's construction, pack an umbrella and sunscreen, and even remember to stash a spare blouse in my purse in case of any last-minute coffee stain emergencies. In fact, I'm so careful to plan extra for every disaster, I arrive at my interview a grand total of forty-five minutes early.

Great start, Hallie.

The Carlisle Publishing building is practically a Manhattan landmark. The huge art deco-style tower looms over its neighbors, with a marble-tiled lobby and an ornate chandelier gleaming off the bronze walls. Inside, I loiter by the main reception, clutching my portfolio and wondering how to kill time, until I see a small gallery space, set in the back of the lobby.

Hello, procrastination.

I wander over and check out the display. Framed photographs hang on the walls, an eclectic collection of photojournalism and art prints, and I browse for a while, curious. I come to a stop in front of a vintage photo of Cary Grant from back in the day, and there's something about the swagger he's throwing off that makes me think of the guy from the wedding. He had confidence in spades too, and a chiseled jawline to boot.

And deliciously kissable lips . . .

I flash back to the moment he reached for me; the hard, lean feel of his body pressed against me, and how his tongue did wickedly sensual things to my mouth. Five seconds, and I was more turned on than I have been in, well, I don't even want to think how long. And sure, he would be the #1 example in the dictionary if you looked up "recipes for heartbreak," but damn, that guy could kiss.

"They're all from Carlisle publications."

A voice from behind me makes me jump. I spin around. It's an older guy, looking like Santa Claus dressed for spring in the city: half-bald with a big white beard, twinkling blue eyes, and a portly belly encased in a dapper linen suit.

"Sorry," the man says, looking amused. "I didn't mean to startle you."

"That's okay." I catch my breath. "I'm kind of nervous. I'm here for an interview," I explain—leaving out the part about hot kiss flashbacks.

"Ah, best of luck. The name's Ernest Hammersmith," he adds. "You're interested in the pictures?"

"Oh. Yes. They're amazing." I turn back to the wall. "I didn't realize how many iconic images were published in Carlisle magazines."

The fall of the Berlin Wall . . . Demonstrators in Tiananmen Square . . . Rocket launches in Cape Canaveral . . . I'm getting seriously intimidated just looking at the record of this place.

"Carlisle publications have always been a window to the world," Ernest says, with obvious pride. "In fact, this very building used to be the tallest in the city, before the Empire State Building was constructed. I curate the collection here, and let me tell you, it's no easy pick."

"I can imagine . . ." I gaze at the images, wondering if I'll ever take a photo that is seen all over the world. I've never thought further than just making a living from my work, but suddenly, surrounded by all these images, I feel inspired to maybe one day join their ranks. "Thank you," I tell him. "This is just what I needed."

Ernest quirks an eyebrow.

"I'm a photographer," I explain. "That's what I'm here interviewing for. Hallie Gage," I introduce myself.

"A pleasure, Hallie," he says. "To tell you the truth, most people just cut through here on the way to the bathroom. It's nice to have someone actually look for a change."

"Their loss," I tell him. "I mean, look at them. You can see the history of the world right here—"

I catch sight of the ornate clock on the wall. For all my planning, I got distracted, and now it's two minutes before noon. "Crapwaffle!" I exclaim. "I have to go. Sorry! And thanks,"

"Good luck!" Ernest calls after me, as I dash back out to the elevators. I hit the button for the twentieth floor, and try to collect myself. It's just the dream job I've been waiting for, the one that will let me wave goodbye to doggie portraits and retirement home boudoir pics (don't ask). Nothing to be nervous about.

Liar. I get off at the editorial floor, and have to catch my breath all over again. It's all glass and glossy white walls up here, with ultra-fashionable people striding around looking purposeful.

I can feel the buzz of excitement, and it mingles with my nerves to make my heart race faster.

"You're late," the receptionist says matter-of-factly when I go sign in. The clock reads 12:02.

"I'm so sorry," I blurt, flustered. "Is there any chance she can still squeeze me in? I won't take up much time."

The girl sighs loudly and clicks through her schedule. "Fine. Over there." She nods

to a row of boxy white chairs outside the corner office, so I go take a seat.

And sit. And sit. And sit.

My stomach ties up in so many knots, I deserve a Girl Scout badge. I haven't seen anyone go in or out, or heard any movement inside. In fact, is she even alive in there?

Finally, a tall, curly-haired woman saunters across the office with a takeout salad in one hand and a Neiman Marcus bag in the other. "Hallie Gage?" she looks around absently, even though I'm the only one here.

"That's me!" I bob out of my seat.

"Oh." She looks me up and down. "I guess you can come in."

I follow her into the office, trying to remember all those power interview tips. Firm handshake. Bright smile. Confidence. I open my portfolio on her polished maple desk.

The editor opens her salad, and drizzles dressing over the top.

"So, I have a degree in photography from RISD," I say, nervous. She pulls my portfolio closer, and begins leafing through with one hand, as the other steadily forks salad into her mouth.

"Mmhm. Mmhm."

That's all she says. I can't even tell if it's an approving sound or a dismissive one. She hardly seems to look at anything before she's moved on to the next spread. I'm not totally sure she can even see past those curls.

I jump in, pointing to a shot over the Hudson River that I'm particularly proud of. "To get that angle, I had to scramble right up on the—"

Her intercom buzzes. "Diane for you on line two."

"Sorry," the editor says, through a mouthful of salad. She swallows fast, and picks up the phone. "Diane! So good to hear from you. Yes, I'm in the middle of an interview, but I can give you a second."

A second turns into a couple minutes of chatter about an ad placement. Meanwhile she's flipped right through half my book. Is she looking at my work or just exercising her hand at this point?

As soon as she's off the phone, I grab the opening. She hasn't asked me any questions yet, so I'll just have to answer the ones I think she should have. "I've loved photography since I was a kid. My grandfather got me my first camera, an old Pentax manual one, and just like that, I was hooked. I know there's a gap in my resume the past few years," I add quickly, "but I've done portrait work, landscapes, commercial—"

Another buzz from her secretary. "Kevin on line one."

She doesn't even apologize this time. "Kevin! So good to hear from you. Did you get those numbers crunched?"

By the time she's done with Kevin, she's reached the last few pages of my portfolio, aka wedding central. I needed to show people have been willing to pay me to point and click.

"Mmhm," she says. This time it definitely sounds dismissive. And that's it. She flips over the last page. Suddenly I really wish I had a doggie bridal party shot to share in there. *That* would get more of a comment, wouldn't it?

I've got to say *something* that'll get her attention. "There was also the time I climbed Mount Everest," I start with a dramatic sweep of my arm. I have no clue how I'm going to explain that line if I have to admit I didn't really. But it doesn't matter.

This time it's Ms. Editor who interrupts. She stands up without so much as a blink, handing my portfolio back to me. "Thank you for coming by, Holly. I'll be in touch."

She's already ushering me out the door. That's it? "Um, it's actually *Hallie*," I say, because damn it, she is at least going to get my name out of this interview. But Ms. Editor is already making a beeline for the new girl sitting outside her office.

And I do mean *girl*. With that artfully tousled high ponytail, cropped jacket, and tapered khaki pants, she looks like she just walked off the campus of the preppiest college that ever prepped.

"Blair!" the editor squeals, putting more enthusiasm into that one syllable than she did our entire conversation. If you could call what we had a conversation. "So good to see you. How are your parents?"

Preppy Girl shrugs with a smile. "Oh, you know, Dad's busy at the office as always. Mom's got her new gala in the works."

Ms. Editor takes her by the shoulder to guild her into the office. "That's right. Is this one for the cancer charity or the lupus charity? I can never keep up. Oh, I'm so glad you took me up on the offer to apply. I have the *perfect* assignments for you."

The door closes behind them before I get to hear all about the assignments she's apparently giving out before even starting the interview. Not that it sounded like any interview was necessary. I bite my lip and turn toward the elevators.

And that's when I realize there's mustard vinaigrette smeared all over my book.

There'll be other openings, I tell myself, trying to stay strong. I'll have other chances. But by the time the elevator arrives, I'm blinking hard to keep back the tears.

I will not cry. I will *not* cry. Not over one silly job.

That I really, really wanted. That I needed.

Shit. I can't even go back to weddings while my camera is doing its excellent impression of a paperweight. Maybe I can start busking on the street? I'll be a mime. A mime photographer. No actual pictures taken. Even a broken camera can handle that!

I'm laugh-crying when the elevator jerks to a halt and the door slides open.

The woman who walks on looks as though she's never shed a tear in her life. The violet silk sheath dress she's got on is perfectly smooth —as smooth as her sleek ice-blond bob. Her eyebrows form two narrow arches. She glances over me and purses her lips. I pray for the floor to open up and swallow me.

Then, instead of giving me a sneer, she reaches into her clutch purse and offers me a tissue. I take it, surprised.

"Looks like you've had a tough morning," she says in a sympathetic voice. "You know what always makes me feel better?"

Botox, I answer silently, then shake my head.

The woman grins. "Donuts."

3

HALLIE

MY KNIGHT in shining silk's name turns out to be Olivia Danvers. "It's my firm belief that there's nothing in the world a good chocolate glaze can't fix," she says, waving her half-eaten donut in the air. She smiles at me from across the formica table of the diner down the block.

"You're right," I agree, not caring that creme filling is probably smeared half-way down my face. "This sugar rush is almost enough to make me forget the mess I made up there."

"Ouch," Olivia says, looking sympathetic. "Who went and stomped on your heart?"

My cheeks heat. "Oh, it wasn't— I mean, it's not something that serious. Just a job interview. I don't know why I got so upset."

"Nothing to be embarrassed about," Olivia says, although I can't imagine *her* crying in public—even if she just got told she had two days left to live. I'm still not sure why this sleek and polished vision of competence decided to take pity on me. Maybe it's her charity work for the day. Either way, I'll take the sympathy—and the Boston creams.

"What kind of job? Are you a writer?" Olivia leans forward on her elbows. I've never met anyone whose elbows looked elegant before, but ladies and gentlemen, this is her. I'd bet even her belly button is a portrait of sophistication.

"No, a photographer," I answer, brushing sugar off my blouse. "At least, I'm trying to be. It's . . . not exactly going to plan. I got mauled by half a dozen rabid shih-tzus yesterday, and the editor barely looked at my portfolio. Like she was just passing the time. Waiting to give the position to some girl who earned it by being a daughter of some important friends." I sigh. "I know it's all about who you know in, well, life, but I figured at least I'd have a shot if someone saw my work. Unless my work *is* the problem." I stop and furrow my brow. "Maybe I've just been kidding myself, and I should go find a portrait kiosk in a mall somewhere to ply my trade. At least I like novelty Christmas sweaters. And babies." Visions of my future dance before my eyes, until Olivia politely clears her throat.

"Here, have another donut."

I take it and flush. Why did I babble all that to her? She must think I'm certifiable by now. But Olivia is watching me thoughtfully. "You clearly lead an interesting life."

"I suppose," I reply. "I mean, that's the artist's life, right? And I don't mean, *artiste*, all pretentious or anything, just, trying to make your own path, do something creative. I did the 'sensible' thing for years," I add, in case she thinks I'm one of those naïve people who woke up one day and decided to live my dreams, to hell with, you know, actually making rent. "I worked in an office, booking meetings and running paperwork, but it just wasn't the same. I wanted *more*. I figured if I didn't make the leap now, I never would. But my safety net is all spent, so I guess I'm face-diving straight into oblivion."

Shut up, Hallie! Oh, God, I sound pathetic. I stuff the rest of the donut into my mouth before I can spill my guts even more.

"It'll be okay," I manage to mumble through a mouthful of lemon filling. "I always bounce back. If I could wrangle Jack Callahan for four years, I can find a way through this."

Olivia's eyes brighten. "Who did you just say you wrangled?"

I swallow the donut. "Jack Callahan. You know, the tech investor? I was his assistant."

"Oh, I'm aware of Mr. Callahan," Olivia says. "I try to stay on top of all the important movers and shakers in this city. Working for someone that influential must be stressful."

Her tone prompts an answer. The way she's looking at me, I suddenly feel as if I'm in the middle of a test I didn't know I'd sat down for. I lick the powder from my lips. "It wasn't exactly a picnic, no. But you learn how to read the person's moods, when to say 'yes sir' and when to tell them they're being a total ass. Once I got the hang of it, there weren't any problems."

"Excellent." Olivia smiles. I must have passed the test, but I still don't know what she was testing me for. Not neatly eating donuts, I'm pretty sure. I've got the powdered sugar all over my sleeve cuffs, too. Damn.

As I brush it off, Olivia reaches into her purse again. This time, she produces a business card: stark black lettering on ivory linen paper. As elegant as she is.

"I think we're both in luck today. Your interview may not have worked out, but I might have a job for you. It isn't photography . . . but it could give you a leg up in the 'who you know' department."

I accept the card and examine the text. *Olivia Danvers, The Agency.* An address on the Upper East Side.

"There's some paperwork you'd need to do before I can explain further." Olivia stands up, tucking her purse under her arm. "If you think you might be interested, come by that address tomorrow."

"I . . ." I stop, confused. Is she trying to be mysterious, or am I just missing the point?

Olivia gives me a graceful little wave goodbye. "Lovely to meet you, Hallie. I hope to see you soon." Then she breezes out the door before I can say a word.

I stare at the card again.

The Agency.

There's no other information on the card, but as I run my finger over the heavy paper, I feel something embossed on the bottom corner—invisible to the naked eye.

It's a heart.

MY FAVORITE CAMERA shop is on the way to the subway stop—if I take a quick detour of about seven blocks. The side trip is worth it. I need to remind myself of my goals. Keep my mind focused on making that dream a reality. Or something like that. I might be mixing up two of the different self-help books I skimmed through after I quit my job with Jack to make it on my own.

The scruffy guy behind the counter raises an eyebrow as I hurry past. I hope he hasn't been keeping track of how many times I've made this pilgrimage in the last few months. I come to a stop in front of one of the glass cases and sigh with pure longing.

Move aside, Hemsworth. Step aside, Hiddleston. The most handsome sight in the world is right there in front of me. Sleek, dark body. A full set of lenses, more megapixels than I'd know what to do with, a processor that's practically magic . . .

Come to mama.

I set my fingers on the glass, ogling the finest camera I've ever seen. I probably look like an orphan in a melodrama peering from a wintry street through a bright restaurant window. Oh well. No one's here to see me except Scruffy Dude.

It's perfect. I *could* take on Mount Everest with that baby. Possibly Mount Olympus too. We're talking mythic scale, all right? All I need to do is cough up seven grand and—

Excuse me while I die laughing.

My phone rings. My heart leaps. Some part of me still believes it could be Ms. Editor calling to say I got the job. Like I didn't hear her giving it to someone else right in front of me.

I check the screen, and that hope goes the way of the dodo. Not anyone from Carlisle Publishing. Not the new boss I was aiming to take on. It's the former boss I walked out on. I wince and hit the answer button.

"Hello, Jack," I say. "What's up?"

"Hallie." He's frustrated. By now I can tell that in just two syllables. His British accent comes out in full force when he's annoyed. "I don't suppose you'd happen to know where the hell the mock-ups from the Faraday presentation got to?"

The Faraday presentation. My mind leaps back into Jack Callahan's office as if I never left it. "Have you checked the cabinet to the left of the elevators, second shelf from the top?"

"I have not." There's a rustle as he strides over. He sighs. "And there they are. Thank you. And I'm sorry for having to ask. My new assistant is terrible."

"How many temps have you gone through so far?" I can't help asking.

"I believe this is number five. Although normally I'd have counted on you to keep track of that. I hope you're having a *spectacular* time at the expense of my wellbeing."

"You survived all those years before I came around." I smile. "I'm sure you'll manage without me now."

"Hmm. I'm glad you're confident about it, at least." He pauses. "But seriously, now that I've interrupted whatever important thing you were doing, how is the photography business? Everything's going well?"

My stomach flips. I can't bear to admit the truth. Not that he'd make me feel bad about it. No, he'd probably insist on *helping*. And that would be way worse.

"Everything's great!" I say, with all the brightness I can summon. "Lots of gigs, some interesting clients." The ones who think dogs make appropriate wedding attendants, for example. It isn't a total lie.

"Best decision you ever made, then. All right, no need to rub it in. I'll go back to stumbling around without you."

I roll my eyes. "You do that."

My heart feels heavy as I put the phone away. I look at the display case.

Jack would buy that whole setup in an instant if I even mentioned it. He'd call up every business he's worked for and talk me up for every possible gig. I know that. But this is *my* dream, and I'm supposed to be pulling it together on my own. It wouldn't be the same if I let someone else just waltz in hand it to me. It wouldn't feel like I deserve any success that came with it.

I tap the glass in front of the camera. "I'll be back, baby. I promise. With a lot more cash in my wallet."

Next time. I don't want to walk into this shop again without a way of taking that camera home with me.

I stew on that thought the rest of the way home. As I set my purse on the counter, I remember my donut stop. I dig out Olivia's card and study it again. She invited me to drop by—and promised it would help with my career.

I trace the hidden embossed heart again, intrigued.

What the hell. What's the worst that could happen?

4

HALLIE

IN NEW YORK CITY, there are brownstones and then there are *brownstones*. The one that holds Olivia's mysterious The Agency is four stories of absolute old-money glory. I swear the carved stone lintels over the windows have their own lintels. A wrought iron fence surrounds the lowest floor. The door looks like solid mahogany. A sweeping set of stairs leads up to it, with marble lion's heads peering at me on either side.

Whatever business this Olivia is in, she's making some serious money here.

I climb the front steps and press the intercom. A soft chirpy voice carries out. "The Agency, who's come calling?"

Interesting greeting. "Hi!" I say, feeling tongue-tied. "I, um, this is Hallie Gage. Olivia told me I should come by about a job?"

There's a brief silence. Olivia did *mean* that invitation, didn't she? It wasn't just some polite brush-off? I bob on my feet nervously. Please don't tell me my one bit of good luck in the last twenty-four hours was a sham.

Before I end up bounding right back down the steps, the chirpy voice comes back. "Sorry about the delay. Please come in, Hallie."

The lock clicks over. I nudge the door open.

The inside of the place looks . . . surprisingly normal. Like someone's home. Okay, a really fancy home, but what else would I expect from Olivia?

There's a main lobby, with vintage-looking marble floors, a huge vase of fresh lilies on the table, and a staircase sweeping upwards, so I follow it to the top, my pumps sinking into a plush cream carpet so thick, I could lie down and take a nap right here.

A petite young woman appears at the top, dressed in a retro-style pencil skirt and silk blouse. Her fawn brown hair is pulled back in a loose ponytail and her tortoiseshell glasses frame inquisitive green eyes.

"Please come right on up!" she says, beckoning. "I'll get you set up with everything. Olivia's on a call, but she'll be out to see you as soon as she can. Oh, and I'm Alice."

She gives my hand a firm but quick shake when I reach the top of the stairs. "You can sit in the parlor."

The room she ushers me into is like something out of a magazine. The vintage French furniture is all upholstered in luxe shades of velvet, with elegant lamps perched on antique tables, and a stunning crystal chandelier overhead.

It looks like Olivia: expensive, and untouchable.

I sit nervously down at one end of the sofa. A clear, crisp voice I recognize as Olivia's filters through the doorway from farther down the hall. I can only make out some of the words.

"Yes, of course. We . . . Every time. You don't need . . ."

"Meow!" The interrupting noise comes from my feet. A large, mangy-looking ginger cat butts against my calf with his head. His skull is hard enough that I hear a *thunk* of impact.

"Hey there," I say. "Try not to leave a bruise."

He peers up at me with bright yellow eyes. It's hard to tell which of the markings on his face are stripes and which are scars. He's not exactly a match for his elegant surroundings. But then again, neither am I.

I scratch gently between the cat's ears, and he immediately starts purring louder than a revving motorcycle engine. He smacks his head into my leg again.

"I get it, I get it," I protest. "More scratching, coming right up."

Alice comes hurrying into the room. "Oh, you met Thor," she says. "Don't mind him. He's our litmus test. Olivia knows which clients to take on from how they treat him." She watches Thor drool happily all over my suede pumps. "Looks like he *really* likes you. We'll just need you to sign this non-disclosure agreement," Alice continues, handing me a clipboard with a few pieces of paper fixed to it. "And then fill out the form underneath. Like I said, Olivia should be out really soon."

She scurries back into the hall to sit down at a majestic secretary desk. I look down at the clipboard.

A non-disclosure agreement? What kind of work *is* this that disclosing it would be a problem?

As I read the agreement, my eyebrows rise. *No mention of any activities arranged through The Agency . . . Any use of information overheard while with the client is strictly forbidden . . .* What kind of activities? What would these clients be doing? So many questions and so few answers.

Well, I'm not going to get any answers unless I sign this. I scan the rest of the contract, but it's standard language I recognize from my years with Jack. Nothing crazy, so I scribble my signature and flip to the form. Ah. More questions, these ones for me to answer.

Thor bumps his head against my ankle, purring even louder. As I write in my name, date of birth, and contact info, Olivia's voice carries faintly into the room again.

"None of our girls would ever . . . That's between you and her . . ."

None of *our girls*? Something about the phrasing sends a prickle over my skin. I glance over the rest of the form.

What leisure interests do you enjoy in your spare time?

Do you currently have any romantic attachments?

How comfortable are you making conversation with strangers?

I blink at the paper. What kind of weird employment question-naire is this? What could my "romantic attachments"—which, okay, I have none—have to do with a job? The uneasy prickling comes back.

"You'll always get the exact amount of time you paid for," Olivia's voice carries. "If she leaves early . . . all activities agreed to in advance."

Wait a second. My face flushes. "Their" girls going off with clients . . . "Activities" paid for by the hour . . .

Is this some kind of escort service?

I drop the clipboard on the table and leap up. I stride towards the staircase, but Alice scrambles out of her chair "Wait!" She leaps in front of me. "Where are you going?"

"This job, it's not for me."

Alice gives me a frantic smile. "Olivia *really* wanted to talk to you herself. I'm sure if there's been any confusion—"

"I'm not confused. I just have no interest in being a prostitute."

My voice echoes, and a moment later, Olivia emerges from her office.

"Good. I don't hire prostitutes." She looks as calm and elegant as ever, despite the fact I'm basically calling her a pimp. Or madam. Either way, the fact I don't even know the right word says I definitely shouldn't be here.

"Fine. High-class call girl, or whatever it is you call it," I correct myself. "No judgment or anything, but it's not for me."

"Hallie." Olivia's smooth voice cuts through my babbling. "Would you please come talk with me just for a minute? I think you'll feel much more comfortable after I've explained. I promise I wouldn't ask you to degrade yourself in any way."

I pause. I've got to admit I'm pretty damn curious now, and what-ever the Agency is about, it's clearly afforded Olivia some pretty sweet digs. "All right," I finally agree, curiosity getting the better of me. "But you're lucky I can't resist a mystery."

The corner of Olivia's mouth quirks up. She motions for me to follow her into her office.

Inside, it's just as beautiful as the rest of the building, with a sleek, modern desk set against a wall of antique bookshelves. In the corner, there's a loveseat and chaise, and Olivia takes a seat there, crossing her ankles beneath her like she's Grace Kelly brought to life.

"Now," she says, "let's talk. The first thing I need to make completely clear is that what we do here has nothing to do with sex. In fact, a client pushing for physical intimacy is strictly against our rules. If one did, the contract would immediately be void and you'd be released without penalty."

"Oh," I say, sagging back in my chair. That's pretty clear-cut. "So what *does* the job have to do with? What's with all the crazy questions on the form?"

She gives me a warning look. "I'll just remind you that everything I tell you now is covered by the NDA you already signed."

I nod. "Top secret, pain of death—or lawsuit. I get it."

"Good." Olivia breaks into a smile. "I apologize for the cloak and dagger routine, but, well, discretion is important here. Tea?"

What? I blink. Olivia is pouring from a china tea set. "Um, sure," I answer, impatient to find out what, exactly, is behind all this mystery.

Olivia passes me a teacup and saucer, then takes a breath.

"Here at The Agency, we solve a problem for wealthy men. Namely, how to find a suitable woman."

I furrow my brow. "You're a matchmaking service?"

"In a way." Olivia looks amused. "But our matches are short-term. And about practicalities, not love. Say you're a workaholic CEO, but you need a date for work functions, one who understands exactly who you need to network with—and why. Or the terms of your trust fund won't release until you're married. Or you're an A-list actor with a wild reputation, and you need to be seen settling down to make that Oscar campaign work. You need the right woman on your arm, and you'll find her here."

"So . . . it's all pretend?" I ask, fascinated. "The women just do a big public show of being their girlfriend?"

"Exactly." Olivia beams at me. "The client gets a date without all the messy romantic attachments, and the women are paid handsomely for their time. Plus, they often find the networking useful for their own careers. Being introduced in high-flying circles in business or the arts can be worth more than any paycheck."

I nod. I've seen for myself how many deals get done over dinner, or drinks at the right club. And with some VIP introducing them . . . It's a ticket to the big leagues. "So, do people actually believe them?"

"Why not?" Olivia smiles. "And most of the time, they have fun," she adds. "I'm careful to only match people who will be compatible and get along, and I'm very selective about the clients we accept. So it doesn't really feel like work at all."

Well, when she puts it like that . . . I can see the appeal. If my old boss, Jack, hadn't been so good at picking up women wherever he went—before he went and fell in love—I could have seen him turning to a place like this for the sake of convenience.

"So . . . why did you ask *me* to come here?" I ask. "Do I really look like the fake girlfriend type?"

Olivia laughs. "There is no type. But personality is very important, and if you could manage an alpha male like Jack Callahan for four years . . . well, that's exactly what I'm looking for. I actually have a client in mind for you," she says. "You're even a little familiar with his business already."

Okay, now I'm really intrigued. "Who?"

Olivia reaches for a file. "Maximillian Carlisle."

I blink. "You mean, like Carlisle Publishing?"

"One and the same," Olivia says. "He needs a girlfriend to accompany him to a family gathering. It's a week-long contract, down in Palm Beach."

A week with the Carlisles of Carlisle Publishing? A spark of excitement runs through me. But still . . . pretending to be some stranger's girlfriend? Is that really something I want to get myself into?

"What exactly would I have to *do* at this family gathering?" I ask, still cautious.

"Make small-talk, run interference, act as if you can't resist him." Olivia smiles. "Everything a normal girlfriend would do."

"Almost everything," I remind her quickly. She laughs.

"Exactly. Why don't I set up a meeting for the two of you?" she suggests. "You can chat it through and make sure you're comfortable. If you don't like him, then I'll find another match. No hard feelings."

I waver. It sounds insane, but insane in a weirdly exciting way. Getting to meet the Carlisle's could be the break my career needs—and this Maximillian would be getting something out of the deal, too. He's probably one of those trust-fund playboys who refuses to settle down, trying to keep his matchmaking mother off his case. I can smile and call him baby for a week if it means getting my portfolio in front of someone who will actually take the time to look at it—without leaving salad dressing all over the pages.

"OK, I'm in," I tell her. "But just for the meeting. He might be a pompous idiot. With halitosis. I'm not making any promises."

Carlisle or not, I'm not going to sign up to be the fake girlfriend to a complete jackass.

Olivia laughs. "I think you'll be pleasantly surprised."

She taps out a message on her phone, and a moment later, looks up. "He's just finishing up a meeting at the Soho Grand. Are you free to head over there now?"

I pause a moment, but I'm already in this now.

"Why not?"

I HEAD OVER IN A CAB, courtesy of The Agency, of course. On the way, I wonder if I'm dressed like a prospective fake girlfriend for a billionaire playboy. How does a fake girlfriend even dress? At least I made an effort, knowing I would be meeting the immaculate Olivia.

In a navy shift dress, with boots and a little swingy jacket, I hope I look the part.

Not that I'm the one auditioning here. No, this Maximillian Carlisle is the one who needs to live up to *my* standards if this arrangement is going to work. And OK, so my standards are basically "don't be a total jackass," but you'd be surprised how many men can't even clear that basic hurdle.

There's a reason I'm single right now.

I sigh. Working for Jack, there wasn't time for any other man in my life. Dates didn't take it too well when he called at eleven p.m., needing me to make last-minute travel arrangements, or summoned me into the office on the weekend for a big business deal. I've had a few off-again/on-again flings, and casual hookups, because they were the only ones who seemed to last with my grueling schedule. But watching both Jack and my big brother, Oliver, fall head over heels last year, I've promised myself that the next guy I date needs to be for real. Someone grounded, and down to earth, who doesn't play games. Someone ready for a mature relationship. Someone I can depend on.

Plus, you know, leg-wobblingly sexy, with a sense of humor, and a sharp mind.

How hard could that be?

Not that a real boyfriend is on the menu today. This arrangement will be completely pretend—*if* the client is halfway tolerable.

I step into the hotel lobby and take the directions to the lounge. It's the middle of the day, and the seats are pretty much empty, save a cluster of Japanese tourists by the door.

"Can I help you?" A hostess glides over.

"Yes, I'm supposed to be meeting Maximillian Carlisle." It's a mouthful just saying it. Poor guy, getting saddled with a name like that. I'm surprised there aren't a bunch of roman numerals tacked on too, just for full preppy measure.

"He's waiting for you in the dining room." The woman looks me over, like she's surprised. Uh oh. I follow her through, my heart already sinking. I didn't ask Olivia how old he was. What if he's barely out of college, and I'm going to look like a gold-digging Mrs. Robinson? Or worse, he could be pushing sixty, and I'm supposed to play arm candy to a wrinkly Hugh Hefner wannabe.

"Mr. Carlisle? Your guest is here."

The hostess deposits me beside the corner table, and the man there rises to his feet, turning at the same time so I can see his face for the first time.

I freeze.

The man staring back at me isn't some college kid—or a wrinkly old man. No, he's a drop-dead gorgeous hunk of manly hotness. Broad shoulders, smiling blue-gray eyes. And a mouth I know —intimately.

"Wait a minute," I say, stunned. "You're—"

"Max Carlisle," says Max, aka the hot guy I made out with at the wedding. "And you must be my new girlfriend."

5

MAX

DESPITE MY REPUTATION, I'm not some love-'em-and-leave-'em lothario. OK, I like to have a little fun, no strings attached. I've got places to see, adventures to have . . . But I never make promises I can't keep—or expect my no-strings fun to get tangled up in my regular life. So the last person I'm expecting to walk in the room is the knock-out photographer from the wedding last week. The one who helped me out of a jam—and kissed me so good I almost went and forgot my own name there for a minute.

This is my new fake girlfriend who's going to save me from a week of family judgment and torture?

Things are looking up.

"I'm Hallie," she introduces herself politely, then narrows her eyes at me. "I mean, in case you forgot."

Forget her? I had to take a half-hour cold shower to get this woman off my mind. And other places.

"If you think you could have slipped my mind, you can't have been very impressed by that kiss," I say, flashing her my trademark charming smile. "Maybe I should take another shot at it."

Hallie just arches an eyebrow. "I heard that's against the rules," she says. "Are you breaking them already?"

"Breaking rules is one of my favorite pastimes."

"Along with making out with strange women at weddings?" she shoots back.

"I don't think you're that strange," I reply, and her lips quirk in an inadvertent smile. Score one for me. "But you have to admit, it seems like a pretty big coincidence, seeing you again. Was the wedding some sort of recon mission, scoping out a prospective client for Olivia? She said the Agency had strict entry criteria, but I didn't figure on undercover temptresses."

"Undercover . . . ?" Hallie echoes, then shakes her head. "What? No! You're the one who interrupted me, remember?"

"Oh yeah, the great cupcake heist," I grin, flashing back to the taste of chocolate frosting on her perfectly sweet lips. Now there's a party favor I wouldn't mind taking home for keeps.

Or at least, a night.

I try to focus. Which is hard, when those lips are currently pursed in suspicion. "You didn't mention you knew Olivia."

"And you didn't mention you were trawling for a fake girlfriend," she replies, with a smile.

"Touché. Although, I wouldn't exactly call this 'trawling.' " I take a seat and beckon the waiter over. "Drinks? To celebrate our new . . . arrangement."

"I haven't taken the job yet." Hallie looks me up and down. "And let's just say I've got plenty of experience with your type of man."

I grin. "What—rich, smart, and devastatingly handsome?"

She counts off her fingers. "You forgot cocky, reckless, and irritatingly fickle."

Okay, I like this girl. She can obviously hold her own, which is definitely going to be necessary when dealing with my family. I don't have time to do a whole bunch of these interviews. Why not take a happy coincidence when it drops in my lap?

And if I can get *her* to drop in my lap before the job is done, so much the better.

"So is your interrogation over?" I ask, ready to get down to business. Once I make a decision, I go all in, and if we're going to figure out this fake girlfriend deal, time's a-wasting. "Because you might want to hear the actual details of the job before you decide I'm an irredeemable wastrel."

"Wastrel?" Hallie laughs, but she takes a seat. "Note to self, you're the dramatic kind."

"Nope." I shake my head firmly. "In fact, this whole thing is my attempt to avoid drama."

"What, do you need more help fending off cougars on the prowl?"

I grimace at the reminder. I'm lucky the mother of the bride didn't try to tattoo her phone number onto the back of my hand. "No, thank God. It's last minute, but important. I'm heading to Palm Beach for my grandfather's 85th birthday this weekend. All my relatives will be there. Which means a nonstop lecture about settling down and starting a family. Unless I already have a devoted girlfriend on my arm." I grin. "Hello, devoted girlfriend."

Hallie snorts. "Given all the stellar qualities you just pointed out to me, you have to have other options. Why not just bat your eyelashes at some girl on the street and take her along when she swoons?"

"Oh, making the girls swoon is not an issue," I reply. "But I don't do long-term relationships, and bringing a real date along to meet the family . . . she might get the wrong idea."

"You mean, that you're a grown adult capable of real relationships?" she says, teasing.

I clutch my chest. "Oh, she wounds me!"

"Like I said." Hallie shakes her head. "Drama."

"Look, I'm just trying to keep my life simple," I tell her honestly. "I'd rather be up front and put all my cards on the table with you than charm some other woman into believing we have a future.

Besides, you haven't met my family. I wouldn't subject anyone to them without a generous payday."

Hallie seems to perk up a little at that, so I lay down my ace. "I'm offering fifty thousand dollars for the week," I tell her, "plus all expenses covered."

This is the part where her eyes go wide and her jaw goes slack before she scrambles to sign on the dotted line.

Except . . . Hallie's not scrambling. She tilts her head to the side, looking thoughtful. As if fifty thousand dollars might not be worth it. To spend a week in my company, on my dime.

I should be offended, except I'm too busy wondering what it would take to change her mind.

"How soon do you need to have an answer?" she asks. "I'm going to need to think about it."

"What's there to think about?" I ask, confused. "It's a paid vacation. With excellent company."

"It's a big proposition," she says. "Upending my life for a whole week. And you *are* technically a stranger," she adds.

A stranger who knows how good it feels to have her curvy body pressed up against me. But I'm guessing reminding her of our *heated* history won't go putting her at ease.

"I'm a teddy bear," I reassure her. "Eight out of ten women find me irresistible."

She laughs. "And the other two?"

"One was gay, the other preferred her guys hairy." I shrug. "Can't win 'em all."

She's smiling now, which is a start. "But what if I fall for your charms and don't want to let you go?" she asks. "That would totally mess up your plan."

She's *definitely* making fun of me now. I just smile. "I get the feeling there's not much chance of that."

The waiter is hovering nearby, so I order the most expensive cognac they've got. He hurries off and returns a minute later with two glasses. The stuff is almost the same color as Hallie's hair. I watch as she peers at her glass and then tips it back.

Now her eyes widen. "Wow," she says. "This is what I'm talking about. Can I get the whole bottle of that to go?"

I arch my eyebrows. "Only if you take the job."

"Resorting to bribery now, huh?"

"Hey, I've got to use whatever leverage I can. You're a tough sell."

"And don't you forget it." She raises her glass, and I clink mine against it, and we both drink. Hallie lets out a blissful sigh that makes my mind go to all sorts of places it shouldn't.

Like my bedroom.

"What if I promise I'll have you making that sound at least five times a day all week?" I propose, not even kidding.

Hallie just laughs. "Mmm, tempting." She swirls the glass and drains the last of the cognac. "I will thank you for the drink, though. That was fucking good. Can't argue with your taste in booze."

Then she stands up. Shit. So much for sealing the deal. I pull my business card out, and slide it across the table.

"Remember, the offer's only open until tomorrow."

"I'll let you know." Hallie nods.

I know I shouldn't mind either way. I'm sure Olivia has a long list of classy, gorgeous women just waiting to take the gig, but after spending five minutes with Hallie, I know none of them will measure up.

With her by my side, I might actually have some fun.

She turns to leave, and I catch her arm. "Think about it," I say, dropping my voice so only the two of us can hear. "I promise, you'll have an experience you won't forget."

Hallie blinks, frozen for a moment. She's close enough to touch, the heat of her body right there beside me, separated by just that clinging blue dress of hers.

A dress that could be gone in five minutes in a hotel room upstairs, if she just said the word.

For a moment, I think I see desire flashing in her eyes, then Hallie seems to collect herself. She steps back. "See, that's the problem, Max," she says, giving me a saucy smile. "Not all unforgettable experiences are a good thing. Some of them are better known as mistakes."

And with that, she sashays away, her hips swinging, leaving me speechless for what might just be the first time in my life.

6

HALLIE

BY THE NEXT MORNING, Max has left me three messages on my voicemail, each one more charming and tempting than the last.

"So, to recap," Jules says. "You have a handsome, rich man offering to whisk you off to Palm Beach for the week, with a fifty grand paycheck to boot? What, exactly, is the problem here?"

I've been asking myself that question since I walked out of the meeting yesterday, but I'm still not any closer to an answer. "I don't know!" I slump over the counter of the kitchen island where we're having breakfast. Well, I'm having breakfast, and Jules is inhaling coffee so fast I think she might have learned how to breathe the stuff.

"It could be amazing, but it could also be a huge mistake. How am I supposed to decide? What would you do, Jules?"

Jules cocks her head. "I'd make a pro-con list and compare. Always helps me. What are the benefits?"

"Well . . ." My mind darts back to Max's irritatingly cocky and yet irresistibly panty-melting smile. "Max is arrogant, but he's also pretty fun. Spending a week with him wouldn't be the worst thing in the world."

Especially if he kisses me again. *Everywhere.*

I shake my head. Olivia made it clear he's not buying *that* kind of companionship. And I've sworn off playboys like him. "I could get to chat up a bunch of people from Carlisle Publishing who might take an interest in my photography. At the very least I'd get a bit of an inside peek at the inner workings there. And, I mean, I wouldn't do it just for the money, but the money is definitely on the pro list. Fifty thousand dollars . . ." I get a little light-headed just thinking about it. "I could rent a studio space, and buy the most incredible camera setup."

"That's a pretty hefty list," Jules said. "And the cons?"

I poke at my half-eaten slice of toast. "Max might turn out to be a complete asshole. And he's already warned me his family is kind of hard to take."

Speaking of things that could be hard to take. In a good way . . .

Down, girl!

"The fact he's so damn sexy could actually be a bad thing," I add. "I'm not supposed to get personal, remember? Plus I could totally embarrass myself and ruin any chance anyone at Carlisle will ever take me seriously. Also . . . Aren't we forgetting the point of the whole thing? Playing at being someone's girlfriend—it's just, well, *weird.*"

"It's not that different from what you did for Jack, is it?" Jules asks. She downs the rest of her coffee and grabs her purse. "I mean, you kept his social life on track, put him in his place when he screwed up, and made sure everything he needed was at his fingertips . . . Playing girlfriend is probably less work!"

She has a point there.

"Whatever you decide, don't let yourself get too worried about what kind of impression *you'll* make," Jules says. "You're awesome, and you're not allowed to forget it. This Olivia woman and Max Carlisle obviously think so, too."

She heads out, leaving me to mull it over as I finish my breakfast. I replay parts of my meeting with Max. The thrill of our quick back-and-forth conversation. The glint in his eyes when he looked at me.

The memory of that hard, hot body pressed up against me . . .

Ahem.

But aside from everything else, something about Max seems like fun. Spontaneous. Adventurous. The kind of good time I haven't had since . . . I can't even remember when. Back when acid-washed denim was in fashion. The first time around.

Don't I deserve a little of that fun in my life?

I'm just cleaning up when my cell phone rings.

"Ms. Gage?"

"Speaking."

"This is Andrea in Human Resources, over at Carlisle Publishing. I'm sorry to inform you that we've filled the photography assistant position with another candidate. Thank you for taking the time to come in."

My heart sinks. Even after that terrible interview, it still hurts to miss out on the opportunity.

"Can you keep me on file?" I ask hopefully. "In case anything else comes up?"

Her tone turns slightly snippy. "We post all our openings on the website, so you'll need to check there for future positions."

My heart sinks lower. "I just meant, if something comes up that you think I'd be a good fit for—"

"Thank you for your time."

Click.

Now what? I take a slow breath, trying to picture the next few months: hustling for job openings, begging Frederico for more wedding work, finding a part-time gig when my savings run out . . .

Lying on a beach in Florida with a hot guy, fanning myself with wads of cash.

It seems like no contest, but if there's one thing I learned from my years in business, it's never make a big decision out of desperation.

I go dig my old camera out of my closet. It's the one my grandfather gifted me, a manual Pentax that uses film. These days, I mainly shoot in digital, but the moment I feel the weight of it in my hand, I know it's time to take a trip down memory lane.

They say after you fall off a horse you should get right back on. So I head over to the place of my last catastrophic fall. Central Park always makes for great photography, no matter the time of year.

I avoid the dogs playing in the meadow—sorry, Rover, I'm not quite over the little lake mishap—and wander to my favorite scenic spots. The statues under the canopy of the Mall. The massive fountain in its courtyard. Then up to Belvedere Castle. It's the middle of a work day for everyone who has a real job, but there's still a smattering of spring tourists, and the gorgeous leafy green of the park.

The light is perfect, the sun beaming in the crystal clear sky. And, oh, there's a couple of squirrels . . . having a very enthusiastic hump. Lucky them. I guess I'll give them some privacy. But I can't help being reminded of my present dilemma.

Max: to hump or not to hump? Er, wait, that's not how I'm supposed to be thinking about the job. To hire on or not hire on?

I still don't have an answer. But as I cross the park again, I find myself drawn to the people after all. That couple sharing an ice cream cone, a little dab on his nose. This couple hugging a tree together, because why not? This couple on the bench . . . I'm not sure it's really kosher for his hand to be that far up her shirt out here in broad day— Ack, and there goes the other one down her jeans. Not just the squirrels that are horny today.

Ah, springtime in the city.

When I'm all shuttered out, I take the subway down to the Manhattan School of Art. An old friend from college works there, and loaned me a pass-card for whenever I need some darkroom time. I slip in behind a group of ripped-denim coeds, and find a quiet spot to develop my roll of film. The pungent smell of the chemicals and low red light send me straight to photo-geek heaven. In the dark, sloshing the paper around in the developer, I lose myself and forget the outside world. Slowly, the images take shape: shadowy lines getting more solid until you can see every detail. And with every new print, I feel more certain: this is what I was meant to be doing. I *am* going to find a way to keep at it, and if the path there maybe takes a detour to Palm Beach . . . well, nobody said it would be simple.

I'm all finished and heading towards the exit when a voice carries after me. A voice so distinctive and familiar it stops me in my tracks.

" . . . when you consider the explosive symmetry of the color combinations, you can never look at a pineapple the same way again."

I freeze. That snooty, vaguely faux-British accent could only belong to one person: Curtis Chambers, the guy I dated in college, who promptly broke my heart the minute we graduated when he took a job in Paris and only decided to tell me it was over after I'd bought a non-refundable ticket out to visit him.

I wish I could say I made the trip regardless, and spent two wonderful weeks eating brie and French kissing hot dudes with accents, but nope. I took the hit, and spent the holidays crying my heart out on the couch into Kraft mac & cheese.

The voice comes closer. Shit. I grab the nearest door handle and fling it open—

Right into a classroom full of college kids. They turn to stare at me expectantly.

"I'm, umm, just auditing the class!" I grab a seat in the back and pray Curtis keeps on walking outside, but no, he has to step into the room.

Double shit.

"Here's our guest lecturer for the afternoon," the professor announces brightly. "He'll tell you all about his career and making it in the real world after graduation."

I sink lower in my seat, praying he doesn't notice me. Is it too late to make a run for it?

Curtis heads to the front of the room.

"This is Curtis Chambers, renowned photographer."

Renowned? Since when?

"Thank you." Curtis preens. "It's always great to pass on the knowledge I've gained through my experiences. And what experiences they are. Just this year, I've done advertising shoots out in Tokyo. Then a trip to Kenya. And a gallery show I have coming up next month. I never know whether I'm coming or going."

Clearly, the years have made him humble and insecure.

I can't take another hour of this, so I slip to the floor and start crawling towards the door. I bang against someone's leg. "Whoops!" I whisper. "Sorry, dropped my pencil." I stay low on my hands and knees, inching towards freedom. If I can just make it out without him seeing me . . .

"Wait, is someone back there?"

The professor interrupts Curtis. I crawl faster. So close to freedom. So close!

"You there, on the floor. Get up."

I do—but I keep my back turned. I'm two feet from the door, ready to lunge to safety when—

"Hallie?"

I freeze.

Just perfect.

I turn, and force a smile, even though Curtis—and the entire class of college kids—is staring at me like I'm crazy. "Hey!" I blurt. "Wow, crazy coincidence. I didn't want to interrupt, so I'll just—" I gesture vaguely and take another step, but Curtis cuts me off, sweeping me into a bear hug.

"What are you doing here? Are you teaching, too?"

"No. Just . . . checking things out."

Curtis turns to the class. "Hallie is an incredibly talented photographer, too." He says it proudly, and it's almost worse than if he'd been patronizing. "What are you up to these days. I'm sure she has a ton to teach you guys, as well," he adds.

Oh, let me think. Escaping angry shih-tzus 101. How to be humiliated by your ex. Living off ramen and beans when you're slowly going broke chasing your dreams.

Sure, I've got a lifetime of valuable information up my sleeve.

My rapidly dampening sleeve.

Dammit. Why do I have to stress-sweat? In cotton!

"I've been . . . fine," I manage to reply, still smiling awkwardly. "Some freelance work. Private commissions. The usual."

"Where has your stuff been published?" Curtis asks. "I'd love to take a look."

"I, well— I haven't gotten into any magazines or that sort of thing," I say, stumbling.

Curtis pauses. "I see," he says, looking sympathetic. "Well, keep at it, I'm sure you'll make it someday."

I could almost gag if I wasn't so busy wishing I could disappear in to the floor. "Yeah," I say. "I'm sure I will. Umm, I won't keep you. Teach hard!"

I finally turn and hightail it out of there before I can look like any more of a failure.

If such a thing were possible.

I make it to the exit and hurry onto the street. Could I have seemed any more like a loser? How is it fair that Curtis Chambers of all people got the flashy star photographer career? Back when I knew him, he was . . . kind of mediocre. He talked a big game, but never had much vision. And now? Apparently, that lack of vision has taken him all the way to the top. While I'm literally crawling around on my hands and knees.

Still, as much as I want to write him off as just another poser, a little voice reminds me he's had four years' head-start on me. He went straight into the industry after college, working as an assistant to other, big photographers. I took the easy route, I played it safe. I figured it was better to do the sensible thing and get a day job, rather than take that leap and pursue my art fulltime.

But sometimes you only get where you want to go by taking that risk.

I fish my phone out of my purse. Max picks up on the second ring.

"Hallie," he says in that cocky baritone. "My favorite cupcake thief. Tell me you're not calling to turn me down."

"No," I say, with a tremor of excitement. "You've got a deal. I'm in."

7

HALLIE

THE NEXT DAY, I look at my half-packed suitcase and despair. "Crapmuffin, he's picking me up in five minutes!"

"So? He can wait," Jules replies.

"Um, I'm on the clock, remember? Official girlfriend duties."

I scramble off the bed and toss a couple handfuls of panties into the suitcase. Pajamas! An extra bra! Should I be going casual chic or dressy formal here? Do I need to bring my own toothbrush or will toiletries be complimentary? So many questions I should have asked. I've been to Palm Beach before, on a spring break trip back in college, but I'm guessing the Carlisles don't stay at the Beachsider Motel, with two-for-one shots on Friday.

There's a knock on the apartment door. Jules goes to answer it while I stuff my essential makeup into a travel bag. The suitcase bulges as I zip it up, and I haul it into the living room in time to hear Jules saying, "So you're the man of the hour."

Max leans against the doorframe, looking gorgeously casual in dark-wash jeans and a simple white button-down shirt, open at the neck. It hits me for the first time just what I'm signing up for.

Me. And him. Playing at being in love. For a whole week.

It's a tough job, but someone's got to do it.

Max gives Jules a charming smile. "The man of the week, unless Hallie's had a change of heart. You're the roommate?"

"Jules Robinson." She offers a lawyerly handshake. "Esquire. Compliments on your contract. Very tight."

Max laughs. "That's not a compliment I'm used to hearing, but sure. Thanks." He turns that delectable smile on me. "Ready to go?"

"As ready as I'm going to be." I say, my stomach doing a dance of nervous uncertainty. "Viva Palm Beach!"

"Have fun, but not too much." Jules kisses me goodbye.

"Don't worry, I'll make sure she does," Max calls back. The sly glint in his eye suggests he meant the "too much" part.

He turns to me and takes in my massive suitcase. "It is a *week* we'll be gone for, not a month."

"I believe in being prepared for anything," I inform him.

Maybe that comes out a little flirtier than I meant, because his smile grows. "My kind of woman."

There's a sleek black town car waiting at the curb outside. The chauffer is already opening the trunk for my bags, and tipping his cap to me.

Not for the first time, I'm glad I have *some* experience living the high life. Sure, it was trailing after my old boss, making sure his life ran smoothly, but I know enough to give a murmur of thanks—and keep my knees together—as I slide into the backseat of the enormous car.

Max slides in after me. Even with the expanse of seat between us, he feels close.

Too close.

I drink in his chiseled jawline and smiling blue eyes, and begin to feel lightheaded. It's just the nerves, I tell myself, trying to pull it together. Focus on the job. The part he's paying you for.

Ogling is strictly extra-curricular.

"So why don't you give me the rundown on this family of yours," I say, pulling out my trusty notebook and a pen. "I'm going to need details if I'm going to make this trip as smooth as possible for you."

Max smiles. "Doing your homework?"

"Just trying to be prepared."

"Ah yes, you're a regular Girl Scout." Max looks amused.

"You said it was your grandfather's birthday?" I prompt, pen at the ready.

"Franklin Carlisle III." Max nods. "It's his eighty-fifth birthday. He's the one who summoned us all back to pay tribute to his genius."

So: cantankerous, old, rich. Got it.

"And what about your parents?" I ask. If I brought a guy home to meet them, Mom and Dad would be all over him in a heartbeat, wanting to find out everything from his high-school GPA to his blood type.

But Max just shrugs. "Mom checked out of the Carlisle duties about the time of the divorce—said it was the one good thing about it. That, and the alimony. My dad will be around, with wife number three. No, wait, four. You'll meet Uncle Kenny, and the awful cousins."

"Your favorite people?" I tease lightly, and he laughs.

"You'll see."

I pause. "And they won't think it's weird that *I'm* showing up out of nowhere?"

Max doesn't seem concerned. "I've been off traveling the past few years. And let's just say I've been known to act impulsively before. Bringing home a mysterious new girlfriend is nothing compared to . . ." He stops, with an impish smile. "Uh, maybe that's a second-date story."

I arch an eyebrow. "According to our cover story, we should be on date two hundred by now."

"Good point." Max grins. "But we'll save my teen rocker phase for another story."

"I'll hold you to that." I wag my pen at him. But despite the very brief debrief, my stomach is still trying out a contortionist act.

My nerves must show, because Max reaches to squeeze my hand "Hey, all you've got to do is follow my lead and act like you're enjoying my company. Which won't be an act at all."

His touch is warm. Firm. Dangerously exciting.

Remember the rules. No hanky panky.

I release his hand. "What time's the flight? We need to leave plenty of time for security, and checking in—"

"We can do that curbside," Max interrupts. "And don't worry about a TSA pat-down. You'll be sipping champagne before you know it. Just one of the perks of flying first class."

THE DELICIOUS DRINKS aren't the only perk. Between the cashmere blanket, full media library, and more legroom than I can shake a toe at, I'm almost disappointed when we touch down in Florida.

The heat blasts me the moment we step out of the terminal, and I shade my eyes against the dazzling sun. Max strides on ahead, effortlessly steering my bulky suitcase, and comes to a stop besides a cherry-red Jeep rental.

"Hop in." He grins at me. "We'll swing through town to pick up a few things for you before you meet everyone."

"As you've already pointed out, I packed plenty. No need to detour for my benefit." I climb into the passenger seat.

"That wasn't exactly a suggestion, so much as a plan," Max says, pulling away from the curb.

His imperious tone makes me pause. "I am capable of dressing myself."

"Not to insult your packing skills, but I think you're probably going to need a *little* more for this week than you're used to."

"Like what?"

"Well, there's going to be afternoon tea, pre-dinner drinks, dinner, the party—black tie, of course—beachwear, sailing, tennis, luncheons . . ."

I gulp. "OK, you win," I say reluctantly. "But—"

"My treat." He answers the question before I even ask it. "Work expenses."

And just as I'm feeling touched he's so concerned about me fitting in, Max gives me a wink. "Besides, can't have my girlfriend making me look bad."

He guns the engine—and I hang on for dear life.

"So, I have a question for you," Max says, as we speed onto the highway.

"Uh huh?" I gulp, watching the scenery whipping past.

"Why did you say yes?"

I look over.

"To me, this whole crazy arrangement," Max clarifies, shooting me a grin. "I mean, not that I don't think I make an irresistible package, but you didn't seem all that impressed when we met."

I didn't? I guess my poker face is better than I thought.

"Well, you said it yourself, you're a tempting proposition," I say lightly. "And the paycheck isn't too shabby, either."

"That your final answer?" Max raises an eyebrow. I pause, but I don't feel like spilling my guts about the failure of my career just yet, so I shrug.

"For now. We'll see if you earn another one later on."

Max chuckles. "Hallie Gage . . . I can already tell, you're going to keep me on my toes."

WE STOP AT A FANCY BOUTIQUE, the kind so posh the clothes don't even have price tags. All the better not to give me a heart attack. The minute we step foot through the gleaming doors, an immaculate sales clerk materializes.

"My girlfriend is looking to update her wardrobe," Max says with a mega-watt smile. "And you look exactly the kind of woman to help her out."

"Of course, Mr. Carlisle," the shopgirl says with a flutter of her Bambi-esque eyelashes. "I'll take care of that for you."

She disappears in back, and I give him a look. "A regular, are you?"

He looks bashful. "No, but I get written up a lot. You know, eligible bachelors, society pages, that kind of thing."

Oh yeah, I know—that Max is tabloid catnip, and I'm supposed to look like I belong on his arm. It hadn't occurred to me before, but there will be more than just his family sizing me up. Every guest at the party—or eager shop clerk—is going to wonder just how I landed this hot, rich, charming man. And sure, my self-esteem is doing just fine . . . but it'll be a lot healthier wrapped in some designer labels.

I look around with new eyes, feeling like I just stepped into my very own *Pretty Woman* fantasy sequence.

Without the escort part.

Kinda.

"So when you said this was your treat, did you have any . . . limits in mind?" I pick up a silk sundress that feels like heaven under my fingertips.

Max chuckles. "Go crazy. I've got to grab a couple of things too, so I'll meet you back here in a while."

Go crazy. Not words you should ever say to a girl in an expensive clothing store unless you're willing to pay the price. Max saunters out, and I'm left alone to survey the possibilities with a massive smile on my face.

"Is there anything special we're looking for today?" the shopgirl asks.

"I don't know . . ." I muse. "How about *everything*?"

I SPEND the next hour ducking in and out of the luxurious dressing room so many times I'm starting to get whiplash. But damn, the clothes here are *gorgeous*. Gowns, flirty day dresses, some frothy little wrap number that I would never in a million years wear back in the city, but here, seems perfect for evening cocktails on the terrace . . . I try it all.

"That looks amazing on you," the shopgirl gushes over a swooping floor-length silk gown in emerald green. "You *have* to get it." I think I can see commission dollar signs lighting up in her eyes.

As I watch her take my armfuls of purchases over to the counter, I feel the smallest pinch of guilt. But Max did say to go crazy. And I wouldn't even *need* a pair of cute boat shoes (plus full sailing outfit) if he hadn't, in fact, suggested I needed to be spending the day on a boat.

Suggested? More like *demanded*, but Max still hasn't reappeared as the shopgirl rings everything up and stacks a mountain of bags beside the cash register. I catch sight of the total, and feel dizzy.

It's OK, I have to tell myself. It's all on his account.

"Excuse me." A haughty-looking woman approaches. "I am *quite* disappointed with the selection of scarves on display. Do I need to speak to your manager?"

"Oh, sorry, I'll see what I can do," the girl squeaks, and hustles off after Ms. Haughty without another word to me. After all, she's gotten her commission now, right?

I grab the bags and meander toward the door. It's hard navigating the maze of racks when I can barely see over the mountain I'm carrying, but somehow, I make it to daylight without tripping over anything.

"Excuse me."

A voice comes from behind me, just as I manage to swing the door open. A hand clamps down on my shoulder and yanks me around, and suddenly, the bags tumble out of my arms and scatter on the ground.

I'm face to face with a hulking guy in a security uniform. And he doesn't look happy.

"Not so fast, madam. " He turns and yells across the store, loud enough for everyone to hear. "Hey, Candice, I've got a shoplifter!"

8

HALLIE

"I LEAVE you alone for half an hour and you manage to get yourself arrested." Max smirks, his blue-gray eyes sparkling with amusement. "So much for the Agency's top-flight vetting."

"Are you ever going to let me live this down?" I groan, emerging from the cell where I've been waiting. OK, it's not so much a cell, as a back room in the security office, but it's my biggest brush with the law since I got pulled over for driving too *slow* in college, and my cheeks are burning up with the shame of it all.

"Hmm, let me think about that . . . Nope!" Max chuckles, then drapes an arm around my shoulder. "Don't worry, I've done hard time too. There was that police precinct in Brazil, the run-in with Saudi Arabian bodyguards . . ."

I slap his arm lightly. "This is your fault! You walked in there like you owned the place. I assumed you had some kind of account set up."

"You know what they say about assuming," Max grins.

"The clerk didn't even *ask* for a credit card. How did you expect me to pay, anyway?"

"I expected you to wait until I got back," Max replies. "I guess I should have known better. You're obviously an impatient type." We reach the Jeep—now with a heap of shopping bags in the back seat. "I see you had no problem listening when I told you to go crazy, though."

"They all looked at me like I was a criminal." I wince at the memory, climbing into the car. I bury my face in my hands. "I thought I was going to get dragged off to jail!"

Max pats my head. "Don't worry. This was just a minor setback. I promise not to tell my family about your criminal past."

Despite his reassurance, my heart beats faster with nerves. "Please don't. It doesn't exactly scream 'perfect girlfriend.'"

"Aww, you'll do just fine." He glances over at me. "Nervous?"

"From what you've said about them, I think there'd be something wrong with me if I wasn't."

"They'll love you," Max says. "They'll wonder how I managed to land such a smart, gorgeous girl, but they'll love you."

I roll my eyes at his teasing, but the sweet words still make my chest flutter.

Remember this is a job!

"I think we should establish some ground rules," I announce suddenly, as we drive along the curving ocean road. Palm trees are swaying, the ocean is glittering aquamarine blue, and it's all so gorgeous and romantic, I need to cling to some semblance of professionalism.

Max groans. "Do we have to?"

"Yes," I say firmly. "We're pretending to be in a relationship, so things could get . . ."

Hot . . . Tempting . . .

"Complicated," I finally decide.

"OK." Max sounds amused. "What did you have in mind?"

"No touching below the waist," I say. "No PDA except holding hands and quick kisses. No tongue. And no talking about our imaginary sex life."

I'm a little too hot and bothered just imagining we have an imaginary sex life.

"Um . . . I think that'll cover it."

"Fine." Max grins. "I promise not to ravish you in front of my entire family."

"Good."

"So, are you ready? Because we're here."

My head snaps up. He pulls off the main road to a massive wrought-iron gate set in a stucco wall. Max gives the security camera a little wave, and the gates glide open. On the other side, a massive lawn stretches at least half a mile to a mansion so huge it could probably cover an entire New York City block. Palm trees bow over the driveway. Sculpted hedges surround cobblestone walking paths. There's a fountain jetting streams of water that's bigger than my entire fucking apartment.

Holy shit. Maybe I'm not ready at all.

Max cruises down the drive like it's nothing. I pick up my jaw and let myself admire the house as we get closer. It's typical southern estate style: white walls, red clay tiled roofs, a massive main building with wings stretching out on either side. I can see the attention to craftsmanship in the arches of the windows and the sculpted columns along the colonnades.

It's not just massive—it's a work of art. And I'm suddenly very happy I packed my camera.

I mean, I knew the Carlisles were rich, but this is something else. Generations upon generations of compounded wealth must have gone into this place. And at least three of those generations are waiting inside to meet me.

Help me, Jules, I think at my way-too-distant friend. *I'm about to get eaten alive.*

Max pulls into a garage that could hold thirty cars—and does hold about a dozen. I'm dazed enough that I don't undo my seatbelt until he's come around to open my door for me. He raises an eyebrow at me, and I snap out of it.

"I'm fine," I inform him, even though he didn't ask. "It's . . . a very nice place."

He laughs. "Not quite up to your usual standards, though?"

I hop out, taking another deep breath. I can do this. All I need is a little time to explore and settle in. "Well, it *could* stand to be a little bigger. And no swans in the fountain? I'm disappointed, I really am."

He laughs. "I'll have to bring that up with my grandfather. Or maybe you can." He steers me toward the inner door. "Right now, if you'd like. We should be just in time for lunch."

My legs stall. "We're meeting everyone *right now*?"

"Probably better to get it over with quickly anyway. I'm not going to promise you they don't bite, but most of the teeth will be directed at me. And you've got a thick skin, right?"

"Uh huh," I answer faintly. At least I changed into one of the outfits from the boutique, a pale-blue Lily Pulitzer sundress that just screams "preppy"—until you get close enough to see the print pattern is made up of tiny penguins. Still, I was hoping for time to relax, refresh, brace myself . . .

I guess Max can tell I'm still a little overwhelmed, because he leans close.

"Let me tell you a secret," he murmurs, his lip brushing my ear and sending hot sparks rushing down my spine. "I'd rather be in some dusty tent in the Saharan desert than about to face these people. So if you're uncomfortable, at least you can know you're not the only one."

Before I can decide what to make of that—or of the bolt of desire that shoots through me at the same moment—a man who's obviously part of the house's staff hurries over to greet us. "Mr. Carlisle," he says, sounding surprised.

"Hey, Phillips. Good to see you. Still rocking the Whole 30, I see."

The man puffs up, obviously proud. "I'm down twenty pounds already."

"Don't let Chef Renauld hear you," Max warns. "He'll be sneaking butter into your kale salad in no time."

"Noted. The others will be pleased to know you've arrived. Along with your guest?" Phillips' gaze lingers on me with polite curiosity.

"My girlfriend," Max declares, draping his arm around my shoulders again. I still can't get used to hearing that, but I guess I better, and fast, as Max is steering me down a long hallway that seems to go on forever, with marble floors and huge French doors leading outside.

I suppose it's too late to make a run for it? Besides, in these wedge sandals, I probably wouldn't get far.

"Try not to look like you're heading to the guillotine," Max whispers.

Ha. Apt. The revolutionaries would have a field day here. The ceiling has to be twenty feet high, with a flowery pattern carved into the crown molding. A runner with a velvety thick pile covers most of the floor. Maybe it's not the people here who are going to eat me alive —it might be this gorgeous monster of a house.

Max pushes me through a set of double doors into an immense dining room. Two dozen pairs of eyes turn to stare our way.

I gulp.

"Hey, everyone," Max says in a casual voice. He makes a motion with his hand that's somewhere between a wave and a salute. "Good to see you all. Please give a big, warm Carlisle family welcome to my girlfriend, my sweetheart, the love of my life, Hallie."

There's silence.

So much for easing in slowly. After that introduction, I'm surprised there isn't a full-blown fanfare and ticker-tape parade.

I raise my hand in a tiny wave. "Hi there."

The silence continues.

"Flora, great to see you," Max ambles over to the table and ruffles the hair of what must be one of his cousins, a goth-styled girl with dyed black hair and thick eyeliner. "Parker, Brad, been working out?" He high-fives a matching set of blond, tanned figures. I can't tell if they're siblings or husband and wife—until I see the kids beside them.

Because who else could have produced the identical children-of-the-corn style little boys?

"Artie, meet Hallie." Max continues his welcome tour with a guy in a sweater vest and a sneer. "And his wife, the lovely Cordelia."

"Hi." I manage a smile. She sneers back.

OK then.

I look around. Spread out around them are assorted older family members I have to assume include Max's dad and stepmom and all the aunts and uncles. And at the head of the table is clearly the great Franklin Carlisle himself. He studies us with sharp, dark eyes set deep in his wizened face. His thin white hair sticks up in wisps on one side of his head as if he got hit by a strong wind and hasn't combed it since. His sinewy hands are clasped together on the table in front of him. He looks not so much like a family patriarch as an aging king holding court.

I've changed my mind. If I get eaten, it's definitely going to be by these people.

"Grandpa." Max reaches him. "Still alive and kicking, then?"

"Last time my doctors checked." Finally, Franklin looks at me and breaks into a smile. "Lovely to meet you. Does this mean my grandson has finally stopped gallivanting around?"

"I don't know about that," I reply, still nervous as hell.

"Of course you do." Max draws me closer, giving a mischievous smile. "One look at my buttercup here, and my wayward days were over."

Buttercup?

I curl my lips into a saccharine smile. "Oh, pooky, you're so sweet." I look down the table. "Isn't he a darling? I'm so happy to get the chance to meet all of you. My Maxie-poo has told me so much about you."

They look about as dumbstruck as Max.

"Maxie-poo?" he murmurs under his breath, sounding ill. I dig my elbow into his ribs.

Franklin snorts. "All right, all right, you love birds. Get yourselves a seat. Or preferably two."

The only remaining available chairs are between sneering Artie and an aunt with a puff of blue-gray hair. Everyone around us is already eating, and a server materializes behind us and sets plates with perfectly cut sandwiches in front of us. I think the chef must have used a ruler to get lines that straight.

The blond sporty duo is sitting across from us. Parker leans forward with a jab of her fork. *Her* plate is a sandwich-free zone, I see. Just a spread of quinoa and kale and . . . is that a heap of seaweed?

"We thought Max was kidding when he said he was bringing someone," Parker says, eying me suspiciously. " How did you two meet?"

Gets right to the point, doesn't she? Not even a hello. But—oops, maybe we should have discussed our cover story before we marched into the fray.

Max opens his mouth. I'm suddenly sure whatever story *he* comes up with, I'm going to look ridiculous in it. Which is fine, this whole situation is ridiculous, but if we're doing that, he's coming down with me.

I give him a little kick under the table and paste my smile back on. "Oh my God," I gush. "It was the most romantic thing ever. We were in Paris—can you believe it?—and our eyes locked standing right there under the Eiffel Tower. We were even eating the exact same crepe: banana and caramel. It was so obviously meant to be. Wasn't it, *mon petit chou?*"

I snuggle against Max's arm with an adoring glance. He manages not to look exasperated, but I think it's a near thing. "It sure was, *mon demi-glace,*" he says, with a French accent I have to admire. Except that he also kicks me back at the same time.

"Paris, huh?" Parker says, with a slight grimace. I'm not sure if she's offended by the corniness of the story or the thought of eating a crepe. Maybe both. "I guess it's no surprise you were off overseas, Max."

"I'm surprised you bother showing up here at all," Artie says with a sniff. "Seems like most of the time you'd rather be anywhere else. Preferably on the other side of an ocean."

He kind of sounds like he prefers it that way too.

Max keeps smiling, but I feel his body tense next to mine. Even though I shoved us down this path, the snarky comments make me bristle. I'm giving him a hard time in fun. His cousins sound like they're looking down their noses at him.

I squeeze his arm reassuringly. He may be an irritatingly cocky playboy, but for this week, he's *my* irritatingly cocky playboy.

Franklin clears his throat. "I hope the presence of your girlfriend means you're putting that wayward chapter of your life behind you," he says. "At thirty, it's about time you stopped running off on wild adventures and settled down a bit."

Max takes my hand, brushes a quick kiss to my knuckles, and looks past me to his grandfather. "Absolutely," he says. "You'll be happy to know that Hallie and I feel the exact same way. Which is why I asked her to marry me this morning. And she said yes."

What?!

9

HALLIE

"ENGAGED?" I exclaim, the second the bedroom door has closed behind us. "Are you serious? I don't remember that being part of the deal!"

Max strolls farther into the room and tosses his bag onto an armchair. "I don't really see how there's much difference between fake girlfriend and fake fiancée," he says with a shrug. "But if you're worried, I promise I'll draw the line before waltzing you up the aisle to be my fake wife."

"This isn't funny!" I feel like my windpipe is closing up. "An engagement is . . . serious! Committed! You saw how they reacted. Like you've officially lost your mind. Which you have!"

"Calm down. It's going to be fine. You're just here for the week, remember? *Mon petit chou.*" Max tugs a strand of my hair playfully. "You know that means 'my little cream puff,' don't you?"

"Well, you called me your beef stock," I retort, still thrown by the engagement twist—and how nonchalant Max is being.

Nonchalant, and sexy.

He crosses the bedroom and sinks down on the edge of the bed.

The king-sized bed, which I realize is the *only* bed in this massive room.

"You better not think we're sleeping together," I declare, even as my brain leaps into that particular fantasy. "Even literally just sleeping. *You* are taking the couch."

"OK, OK." Max grins. "Come on, admit it was just a little satisfying seeing the looks on their faces after I made that announcement."

I might not know much about his family yet, but I know enough that a tiny part of me enjoyed their shock. While the rest of me was completely freaking out. "Just a little," I admit.

"Anyway, you deserved some payback. That Paris story?" He chuckles. "Next thing, you'd have had me diving in the Seine to rescue your hat."

"Good plot twist. I'll remember that for next time."

My anxiety must still be showing, because Max's smile softens. "How about I give you some Carlisle-free time to get settled?" he suggests. "Take a breather, explore the place, get acquainted. I'll find you later."

I give a grateful nod. We've gone from zero to, well, a dozen zeros at the end of a check in what feels like no time at all, and I need time to wrap my head around it all. "That sounds perfect."

"Don't get lost," he says, on his way to the door. "If you need, just ask Phillips for a map."

The crazy part is, I can't even tell if he's joking. But when he steps out, I've got nothing left to distract me from the wild situation I've walked into.

I'm going to have to spend a whole week with those people. Acting as if I'm head over heels for Max—okay, maybe that part won't be *so* hard—and pretending I don't notice the many barbed comments directed our way. The sizing up and the sneers. I'm not getting any "Welcome to the family!" vibes here.

I look around for my suitcase to start unpacking, only to find it stashed neatly in a closet. Empty. Meanwhile, somebody's already steamed and hung my new purchases in the dressing room, and filled the ornate dresser with . . . yup, my underwear: now perfectly pressed and folded in tiny lacy squares.

I sink on the bed and look around. The guest suite is the size of our apartment back home, with lavish furnishings and French doors leading out to a veranda with a view all the way down the acres of lush lawn to the ocean. I can even see the pale sandy curve of a beach —empty, private, Carlisle property—and a couple of boats bobbing by the jetty. And when I say boats, I mean freaking yachts.

Can I just hide in here for the next week?

I take a deep breath. A plan. That's what I need. I signed up for wild and adventurous, after all. These twenty-four carat judgmental people are part of the deal. I just need to figure out how to handle everyone . . .

And *not* handle Max.

I grab my phone and call Olivia, pacing the polished floor while the phone rings.

"Hallie!" Olivia's smooth voice answers. "You must be in Palm Beach by now. How's it going?"

"He's decided we're engaged," I tell her. "Also, his entire family seems to make a hobby out of biting people's heads off."

Olivia sounds amused. "There's a reason our clients turn to the Agency. It is a job you signed up for, however unconventional."

I flop on the bed. Fuck, that is the coziest mattress I've ever had the pleasure of setting my back on. Would it *really* be so bad if I spent the whole week in here? "I don't know, Olivia. I've never done anything like this before. It's way more intense than I was expecting."

"You'll adapt," Olivia says, reassuring. "And you *have* done this before. How many times did you run interference for Jack Callahan? How many pushy business partners did you have to talk down? You've got this."

Her confidence is infectious. She's right. I've handled way worse than some snooty relatives before. This situation feels different because they're all judging me, too—but it seems like they treat family like business anyway. I just have to think of it like that, and I'll be fine.

"Okay," I say, taking a deep breath. "I can do this."

It's only a week, after all.

My newfound confidence gives me enough confidence to propel me out of the suite. After all, this is going to be the only time in my life I get to enjoy such over-the-top, billionaire luxury. I may as well soak in every solid gold minute of it.

I grab my vintage camera and stroll down the cavernous hallway and out onto one of the verandas. Up close, the detailing on the columns is impressive, and there are even marbled patterns inlaid on the edge of every path. I snap photos, meandering down the steps to a huge, sparkling pool that makes me incredibly glad I brought my bathing suit. It's watched over by two sculptures that look as though they might have been imported straight from ancient Greece.

Then it's on to the gardens. Maybe I should have changed into sneakers? Never mind, the gorgeous scent of roses distracts me from my aching feet. There's a whole tangle of rose bushes, crawling across a lattice far above my head, and a neatly trimmed spread of hedge sculptures.

Yes. Sculptures. In the hedge. I snap a few of them, admiring the detail work, before I catch on to the theme. They're famous historical figures. That one's a hedge-y Winston Churchill. This one a leafy Abraham Lincoln. I think the shapely one next to him is . . . Cleopatra?

The things people decide to do with their money. You think Franklin ever lay awake as a boy, dreaming of the day he could order people to carve historical figures into boxwood bush?

I'm distracted from the topiary by a faint clanging of discordant music. I find Flora leaning against a majestic willow tree, earbuds in and sketchpad in hand. She glances up from her drawing and gives me a crooked smile.

"Hey there, newest almost-family-member," she says, popping out one of the earbuds.

She sounds almost friendly, which is officially the warmest welcome I've received so far today. "Hi! I didn't mean to interrupt."

"Nah, it's fine. Can't blame you for wanting to get away from the rest of those vultures."

"Vultures?" I repeat.

She gives me a crooked smile. "I'm sure you didn't miss the tensions around the lunch table. Let me tell you what no one else probably will: It's got nothing to do with you. Everyone's freaking out about their inheritances. There's a rumor going around that Gramps had his lawyers change his will. And the big birthday event seems like exactly the time to announce the change."

Ah. That explains a lot. So normally they're more like mako sharks than great whites? No wonder Max wanted a girlfriend-shield for this particular get-together.

"You don't seem that worried," I notice.

Flora lets out a cackle. "Right, because I'd make a great CEO. If the rest of my family wants to squabble over Gramps's bones before he's even dead, I'm happy to leave them to it. And they call me morbid because I like to *draw*."

She waggles her sketchpad, revealing a very detailed skull twined with thorny vines. It's very striking in an, er, morbid kind of way.

"I guess I'll just have to stay out of the way too," I say.

"That's the spirit. Just imagine you're stuck in a social experiment gone wrong and try to enjoy the chaos. It'll all be over soon."

She pops her earbuds back in and leans over her sketchpad. Well, at least there's one person here who isn't looking for a feeding frenzy.

I keep strolling, glad at least I know the reason that everyone is on edge.

"Ugh!"

"Argh!"

"Gah!"

I stop. The grunting noises coming from the other side of the bushes are loud and energetic. I should probably turn back the way I came and leave whoever they are to their . . . afternoon workout.

"Crush him!" a female voice suddenly yells. "No mercy, babe!"

What the?

I clear the gardens and find myself looking at an epic battle of vicious determination.

Aka, a game of family tennis.

The court is set up like something out of Wimbledon, complete with umpire's chair and a changing hut nearby. On the grass, Max is facing off against Brad, resplendent in tennis whites that make them both look like bronzed Greek gods.

Or something like that.

I try not to drool, but I can't help noticing that sweat-damp tee-shirt clinging to Max's chiseled chest and the sheen on his muscular arms as he swings the racket. His jaw clenches as he slams the ball toward Brad. And it's hard not to notice the flex of his ass as he charges across the court to return a shot.

I fan myself, flushing. Wow, this Florida heat isn't playing around.

"You've got him!" Parker yells from the sidelines. "Go for the kill!"

Brad nods, and sends a powerful serve smashing down the center line. Max lunges and manages to return. He's playing like his life depends upon it. Actually, they both are. I've never seen tennis this intense. And I've watched the national championships.

They pause to drink some water and change sides. Brad and Parker lean in for a pep talk, then slap their palms together. "Three, two, one, WIN!" they chant. Max sees me and saunters over.

"So this is what you people do for fun?" I ask, snapping a photo of him. For, um, professional purposes.

"When in Rome . . . And I like a challenge." He winks. "How about a kiss for luck?"

I flush harder, but it is part of my official job description, so I lean up and land a quick peck on his cheek.

"That wasn't the kind of kiss I was talking about," Max says, with a smoldering look. "But we'll pick up later."

He heads back on court, and maybe I'm his lucky charm, or maybe Brad's muscles get in the way of his swing, but Max steals the next points and wins the whole game.

"Woohoo!" I call, while Parker scowls.

"One win out of five games," Brad says with a shrug, but he looks a lot madder than he's trying to sound.

"Guess I just needed some time to warm up," Max grins. He strolls over to me. "So how about that victory kiss?"

He pulls me close, but I duck out from under his arm, flustered. "Why don't you show me the rest of the estate? I've walked around, but I bet I'm missing something."

Max seems amused. Sweaty and rippling, and amused. "Sure thing, pookie-bear."

He offers me his arm like an old-fashioned gentleman. "Tough break, Brad," he calls back, to where Parker is berating him in a whisper-hiss. "Work on that backhand, why don't you?"

"He'll probably be out here practicing all night," I murmur, as we head away from the court.

"I don't doubt it." Max shakes his head. "Those two take 'competitive' to a whole other level. You know, when we were kids, we used to have a big family Olympics every summer: tennis, sailing, swimming. The winner got a trophy and everything. Until Parker started sabotaging all her competition. We had to cancel the year she left broken glass on Artie's bedroom floor; he was in stitches all summer."

"Seriously?" I blink. "Wow, that's extreme."

"She was ten at the time," Max adds.

I laugh. "Remind me never to cross her."

Suddenly, Max takes my hand and pulls me off the main path, ducking through an arbor and towards a low, windowless building.

"Where are we going?" I ask breathlessly.

"My favorite place on the whole estate," Max says mysteriously. He leads me to a door, and I follow, wondering what OTT extravagant luxury is waiting on the other side. Indoor circus? Twenty-foot Jacuzzi? Endangered species petting zoo?

Close enough.

We step into a vast room with gleaming floors, containing . . .

"You've got to be kidding me."

I look around, amazed. We're surrounded by pretty much the most gorgeous vintage cars on the planet—row after row of sedans and convertibles, and— My head is spinning. Lamborghini, Cadillac, Aston Martin . . .

"This is insane!" I exclaim, trailing my fingers over a polished hood. "I'm not even a car person, but these are works of art."

"Right?" Max says. A pleased glow has come into his face. He walks between the cars, looking over them like a kid in a toy store. "This was always my favorite part of the estate when I was growing up. My grandfather would come out here with me, and show me how to work on his new acquisitions. He taught me how to take apart an engine—and put it back together again, although that part's harder."

I think of the Franklin Carlisle I met at lunch today. "Are we talking about the same person? I can't imagine him getting his hands dirty."

Max smiles ruefully. "He's cantankerous and a little crazy now, but he was good to me when I was a kid. I could count on him more than my dad. *He* was busy going through wives number two and three."

"It seems like Franklin isn't thrilled about your current hobbies," I note, remembering the comments at lunch. "Especially the whole traveling thing."

"No." Max sighs. "He'd rather I stayed close to home, took my place on the company board and ran things here. But I don't want to be stuck behind a desk. The traveling isn't just a hobby, it's my job," he explains. "I report for some of our news magazines and papers. I really *was* in the Sahara. And Turkey. Uganda." Max gets a spark of excitement in his eyes, then looks around. "And then I come back here, and it's like a war zone in miniature. Good times."

His tone is dry, but I know I didn't imagine his reaction at lunchtime. He wishes his grandfather respected his work more—and the rest of his family too.

I feel a surprising pang. Max may come from this life of unbelievable privilege, but my family have never been anything but one hundred percent supportive of my photography.

"I'm sure he's proud, in his way," I say encouragingly. Max gives me a look.

"He just cares about the bottom line these days. Which my reporting only helps. I've brought in a bunch of big exclusives that really helped circulation, but, I guess he doesn't see it that way. But he's getting old, he sees things a certain way." He shrugs. "I try to cut him a little slack. The others? I just pummel them in tennis."

I laugh. "And you do that so well."

"Glad you appreciated the show." His smile turns smoldering, and I wonder if my ogling was really that obvious.

I clear my throat, flustered. "So, which one of these beauties is yours—" I start to ask, until

my foot skids out from under me. I yelp and throw out my arm to try to catch myself.

A second before my butt hits the floor, I hit Max's arms instead.

"Careful there," he says, easing me back onto my feet.

For a moment, I'm crushed against the solid heat of his body. So close, I can feel his breath, hot on my cheek. So close, I can feel all those muscles I was admiring earlier today.

So close, I could just lean in and *kiss* him.

I don't know if he can read my mind, but suddenly, Max's lips are on mine. Hot, and slow, and dangerously sensual.

Oh my God.

And also, *yum.*

I kiss him back, lost for a moment in the surge of heat, and how damn delicious it is to be back here again. The wedding was like an appetizer, compared to the slow, thorough exploration Max's tongue makes of my mouth, teasing deeper, stroking against me and making my whole body weak with—

Something clatters to the ground, bringing me out of the moment.

What the hell are you doing, Hallie?

I come to my senses just in time, and pull back, flustered. I'm pretending to be his fake fiancée here. Emphasis on fake!

"Sorry!" I blurt. "I, um, don't know what came over me."

"I know what could be under you," Max says, reaching for me with a hot look in his eyes.

Damn. Double damn.

"No! Thank you." I leap back. "I mean. This *arrangement* is complicated enough. We should probably not do that again. You know, for clarity."

Max blinks.

"It's just pretend," I add, my heart racing in a very not-pretend way. "Our engagement. We don't want to blur the lines."

"No, of course not," Max exhales. "You're right. Here, you've got . . ." He brushes down my wrinkled dress, and his hand seems to linger on my waist just a few seconds longer. The touch of his fingertips burns through me, and for a moment, I think about throwing caution to the air-conditioned breeze, hopping up on the hood of one of these gorgeous cars, and begging him to take me now.

Real professional, Hallie.

"Ready for round two?" Max asks, and my brain snaps straight to that kiss. Yes please. And rounds three, four, and five . . .

"You know, the big birthday party tonight," he adds, and I try to scrape my mind out of the gutters.

"Oh. Yeah. Define ready?" I say, wincing at the thought of facing the entire Carlisle clan—plus a few hundred movers and shakers for good measure.

"I've got your back," Max promises. "Besides, you're my fiancée now."

"Don't remind me." Now there's an even bigger spotlight shining on me, the interloper. And despite his kidding, I don't want to let Max down.

I'm here to do a job, and I can't let his gorgeous mouth distract me. It's time to show these back-stabbing, ultra-competitive, totally judgmental people what we're made of.

Ah, family.

10

HALLIE

THE NEXT DAY is thankfully low-key, with just a tense family breakfast before everyone breaks off to do their own thing. Max disappears to work on a freelance article, and I spend the day lounging on the beach before heading back to get ready for the big party. I picked out a floor-length sweeping gown in the boutique on the way over for tonight's big event, but looking at myself in the mirror with only minutes to spare, I'm struck with nerves. Is it too much? Or maybe not enough? From the way Max described the party tonight, it's more like a red carpet gala, the Oscars meets a Presidential Inauguration—with the guest list to match.

And I'm supposed to blend right in. Ha. As Max's one true love. Double ha.

The door swings open, and my supposed fiancé comes barging in without so much as a knock. "Hey!" I protest. "For all you know I'm naked in here!"

"I . . . uh . . ."

Max is stammering uncharacteristically. I turn. He's staring at me —the kind of slow, heated stare that makes me flush from head to toe.

He lets out a low whistle of appreciation. "Wow. You look incredible."

"Thanks." The fabric felt cold when I put it on. Now my skin is sizzling. Max is looking pretty wow himself. His usually-ruffled hair has been tamed smooth, and that divine body of his fills out his fitted tux to perfection.

"Well, don't you clean up nice?" I say, trying to pretend the heat I'm feeling isn't desire.

Florida. Too humid by half.

Max strolls over all casual, but I swear I can feel the temperature rising with every step he takes. He dips his hand into his pocket and produces a ring box.

I blink at it for a few seconds. "Um . . ."

"We're supposed to be engaged," he says. "And I figure my betrothed deserves a ring."

Right. The act.

He pops the box open, and I can't help gasping. The ring inside is literally the most beautiful piece of jewelry I've seen in my life. A massive, sparkling diamond sits at the center of a spiral of smaller stones, shaped like the unfurling petals of a rose. As I gape at it, Max takes my hand. He slides the platinum band onto my finger. "A perfect fit."

"Meant to be, obviously," I joke faintly. But I'm still a little awed as I hold up my hand in front of my face. A rainbow of colors glitters inside the finely cut gems.

I never imagined I'd wear anything this gorgeous—or this expensive—even for pretend. "What if I lose it?" I gulp. "Or get mugged?"

"In the Carlisle ballroom?"

"You know what I mean!" My heart races, just trying to imagine how much money is currently sitting pretty on my ring finger.

Max chuckles. "Relax. There's security at every exit. And all the family gems are insured."

"This is an heirloom?"

"Of course. A Carlisle would never be gauche enough to propose with a store-bought ring." Max's tone is mocking, another glimpse of that family responsibility he carries around.

"Oh. Well, thank you. It's beautiful."

"As are you," he says smoothly.

I slip into the bathroom to collect my earrings, but when I emerge, Max is by the desk, leafing through a familiar-looking portfolio. "Are these your photographs?" he asks, looking up.

"Where did you—?" I stop. Of course. Whoever helpfully ironed my panties must have unpacked the portfolio, too. "Umm, yes."

"These are good." Max furrows his brow. "Really good. Have you thought about getting published?"

"Ha!" I snort with laughter. "Only every day since art school." I drift closer, wondering if he's just being polite. "You really like them?"

"I do." Max lingers on one of my favorite prints, a misty morning shot of the meadow in Central Park. I found a woman sitting on the bench there alone, just gazing at the trees, and something about her solitude hit me right in the chest. "It feels like she's the only woman in the world," he says quietly, and I'm surprised that someone as charismatic and charming as him could even recognize what loneliness looks like.

"We shouldn't keep everyone waiting." I quickly take the book from him and put it aside.

Max gives me a look. "Foiled again." He offers his arm. I collect my jeweled clutch purse and take it, balancing on my stacked sandals as he steers me out of the room.

"How many people are going to be at this thing exactly?" I ask, trying to calm my nerves.

"Oh, only several hundred or so."

My stomach flips over, and I try to give myself a quick pep talk. I've got this. I've been at huge conferences with thousands of important people. So what if I'm the one on display this time? They don't really know me. I'm just a future Mrs. Carlisle to them. Here for Max, not myself.

This is business, not personal.

BY THE TIME Max and I make it across the estate to the ballroom, my feet are killing me. "You guys should have golf carts to get around," I joke, trying to ignore my jittery pulse.

"I'll put that in the suggestion box."

We step into the ballroom, and my breath catches.

The ceiling here has got to be two stories high. Massive chandeliers dangle from it, their light shining off the gold leaf decorations. The place is big enough to feel like I've just entered a football stadium. A very, very well decorated football stadium. With a hell of a lot of people in it.

I don't think Max was exaggerating when he said "several hundred." They're swarming in clusters all around the room. All of the women are in dresses as elegant as mine, the men in starched tuxes or the fanciest of suits. Their voices bounce off the ceiling in a mishmash of sound.

"It's showtime,"Max murmurs, sounding reluctant, and I'm reminded that I'm here for him, not me. My nerves don't matter—what does is making tonight as stress-free and easy for him as possible.

"Never been more ready," I reply brightly, and squeeze his hand. "Let's knock 'em dead. Metaphorically speaking. Although, I'll be on the lookout for Parker coming at you with the butter knife."

It works. Max gives me his trademark smile. "Never turn your back on a Carlisle," he quips, and we wade into the fray.

We don't make it more than a few paces before someone grabs my arm. "Oh!" exclaims a stately woman with a small beehive of silver hair. "You must be the new fiancée I've been hearing all about."

"That's me!" I say brightly. "It's so exciting to be here and meet so many of the people in Max's life."

She looks down her nose at both of us. "Well, I'm sure we'd be a lot more in his life if he were *around* a lot more. Where were you gallivanting this time? I do hope this means he'll settle down now," she adds to me. "Being a Carlisle isn't all jet-setting vacations, you know."

Max gives a measured smile. "I contribute in my own way, Aunt Diane."

She makes a snorting noise. I grasp Max's elbow. "What was it you were telling me the other day about how your reporting increased readership?"

He looks a bit puzzled, but he follows my lead. "That's right. We actually saw subscriptions increase by fifteen percent last year after I started my regular reporting for Global Weekly, for example."

"Oh," the woman says, looking genuinely taken aback. Apparently there's no way she can belittle that accomplishment, so she brushes it aside. "Well then. I just hope you'll consider taking your seat on the board before too much longer."

"Seat on the board?" I whisper to Max as he pulls me away.

"The board of directors for the company," he says. Right, of course. "We're all supposed to attend. But like I said before, sitting at a desk, even a big one, doesn't really appeal."

"OMG, look at the size of that thing!" We're interrupted as a gaggle of ladies comes over to ogle my ring. Playing along with their oohs and ahs is easy enough. I grin and giggle and fawn all over Max like any adoring fiancée would. "I don't know *how* I got so lucky," I gush. "I just know we're going to have a wonderful future together."

Max snickers, and I jab my elbow into his ribs. "Roses are my favorite flower," I add loudly. "So he found the ring to match. Isn't that sweet?"

"Is that true?" Max asks, after we move away. "About the flowers."

"Nope." I grab a glass of the finest wine I've ever had the pleasure of pouring down my throat. "I'm more a daisy girl myself. But now your proposal is even more special."

"I don't know if I should be impressed or worried at how easily you lie," Max murmurs.

"Definitely impressed."

A portly man who I swear has a monocle tucked in the breast pocket of his suit comes sauntering over. "Young man, young man," he says, clapping Max on the shoulder. Max winces. "It certainly is good to see you finally settling down. I hope you're going to apply the same philosophy to your career now."

"I haven't made any decisions about that just yet," Max says.

Geez, these people really are singing from the same hymn sheet, aren't they?

"Oh, but I'd be so sad if you stopped with the reporting." I turn my oh-so-innocent gaze on Portly Dude. "The work he does is so important, you know. Bringing awareness to all those global crises. Encouraging accountability on an international scale. How could there be a more worthy cause?"

This dude obviously can't think of any. He blusters wordlessly for a moment and then just says, "Keep in mind where you're meant to be."

Max chuckles as the guy waddles off. "Very smooth, Hallie. Very smooth." He gives me that thoughtful look again, but it feels warmer this time. Almost tender. Or maybe he's just acting the part too. "Thanks. It's funny, it never occurred to me that having a fiancée might mean having someone on *my* side for once."

"I guess you'll just have to get used to it," I say instead, walking my fingers teasingly up his chest. Something hotter sparks in Max's eyes, and suddenly, the room seems smaller. More intimate. Like we're the only two people around.

I look away. "Where to next?" I ask loudly, taking another gulp of wine.

"You haven't met Uncle Kenny yet." He slips his arm around my waist, and directs me across the room. "He's one of the good guys."

Even if he hadn't told me that, I could still have guessed from the way Kenny raises his glass to us in greeting. "I hope you kids are having fun," he declares. "Because I definitely am not."Max laughs. "No one makes you come to these things, Uncle Kenny."

"Oh, you know the fuss the old man would kick up if I didn't. Anyway, I've got to stay in touch with things, see what's in style."

"My uncle is the art director for Carlisle Publishing," Max says to me in explanation.

My heart leaps. Then he's the guy who's the boss of the boss of the boss of that editor who couldn't be bothered to look at my portfolio. It's a shame I couldn't have snuck that big binder in here under this dress.

"It's a pleasure to meet you," I say.

"The pleasure is all mine," he says with a tip of his head. "I'd welcome you to the family, but, well, you've met them, so it would be more of a condolence."

"I'll take it anyway," I smile. "Max says you're one of the good ones."

"He does, does he?"

"Don't let it go to your head," Max adds. Kenny laughs.

"We like to stick together. And now our numbers swell, with you. We'll have them beat in no time."

He turns to greet a passerby, and I touch Max's arm lightly. "Can you point me to the bathrooms—or do I need GPS?"

Max chuckles. "Just keep heading to the back of the room, then take a right."

"Thanks."

I slip away, and manage to navigate to the opulent bathrooms without any major mishaps. Inside, I splash water on my wrists and take a deep breath. So far, so good. I'm not humiliating Max, at least, and it doesn't hurt that snuggling up to my beloved fiancé isn't exactly a chore.

Who's turning out to have way more depth than I gave him credit for . . .

Not that it matters to me. I freshen up my lipstick and head back out, taking my time to absorb the crowd. *A social experiment gone wrong*, Flora called this whole to-do. It's a hell of a spectacle, that's for sure.

A familiar nasal voice reaches my ears. "I've been putting the pressure on him for *years*. It's ridiculous the way he's holding out."

Cousin Artie is holding court just beyond the bar, his lips pulled back in their typical sneer. "My grandfather has no sense of the times. The company is a dinosaur. We should sell it off while there are people still wanting to buy it."

"Right," a guy beside him laughs. "Like Franklin would ever agree to that."

"I'm going to keep working on him. I've got several of the key board members backing me up. But he owns too much of the stock to do it without his go-ahead. Parker's been nudging him too. We'll see."

Lovely. Now I definitely don't feel guilty about thinking of the family as sharks. What a bunch—Franklin Carlisle lording it over everyone in his slightly maniacal way, the younger generation circling him, ready for a feeding frenzy.

Really, it's a miracle Max turned out as grounded as he is. And when I'm thinking of a cocky billionaire playboy as fucking *grounded*, you knew these people are the next level of bizarre.

"There you are." Max's arm slips around my waist. "I was ready to send up a distress flare."

"Your fan club getting to be to much?" I say lightly.

He snorts. "More like the Disappointment Society."

"Well, this fan club member thinks you're doing just fine." I give him a reassuring smile, just as Franklin emerges from the crowd near us. He manages to look imposing even though that skinny frame can't weigh much more than half what I do. If he combed his hair before the party, you can't tell. He has put on a tuxedo, though—a deep purple number that matches the . . . is that a gold dragon's head protruding from the top of his cane? Yes, yes it is. With glinting amethyst eyes.

All righty then. Throw in a cackle and he'll have the supervillain part nailed.

"Grandchildren," he says with a broad sweep of his arm. "A word, please."

From Max's expression, I can tell what we please doesn't matter much at all. He takes my hand, and we troop after the old man. Artie stalks along too, catching up with Cordelia along the way.

We duck into a side room that's just as lavish as the ballroom we just left. A grand piano stands at one end, at the edge of a Persian rug. Flora, Parker, Brad, and their parents are all already assembled. We come to a stop beside Flora.

"What do you think the big announcement is?" she asks. "We're all getting ponies?"

Max chuckles. "Somehow I have a feeling it's not going to be anything that simple."

Franklin takes his place at the head of the room, and a tall, dour-faced man motions for silence. "That's his lawyer," Max murmurs. His hand tenses around mine. Yeah, even I can figure out that's probably a bad sign.

Franklin clears his throat. Like magic, every murmur in the room falls away. All eyes rest on him.

"Thank you all for joining me here to celebrate my eighty-fifth birthday," he says. "Though I don't fool myself into thinking any of you really *want* to be here. Which is exactly why I feel it's time I made a few changes. Percy?"

The lawyer moves through the room. He hands each of the blood relatives a sealed linen envelope. Max turns his over in his hand, frowning.

Franklin waves his cane at his assembled family. "I'm shaking things up around here. You're all lazy, irresponsible layabouts. So, forget cashing in on me when I leave this mortal coil. You want to inherit the company? You're going to have to earn it. Prove you've got what it takes to carry on the Carlisle legacy."

"Dad, what are you talking about?" Uncle Arthur says. He's gone very pale.

Franklin gives him a thin smile. "We're going to have a treasure hunt. Or rather, *you're* going to have a treasure hunt, and I'm going to watch. Each of you has the first clue in your envelope. The first one to the end of the hunt wins it all." His eyes twinkle. "Every last share I own. It'll all come down to one of you."

11

MAX

IF THERE'S one thing my grandpa loves, it's a scene. And man, does he get one. There's a moment of shocked silence as his words since in, and then the room explodes in bedlam.

At least half the room is shouting, but my cousin Artie is yelling the loudest. "This is ridiculous!" he cries, waving the envelope. His normally pale face has flushed red as a candy apple. He marches up to Gramps with Cecilia and Uncle Arthur in tow. "There's no way this is legal. I'm calling my lawyers—all of them! You're insane. You can't change a will under that condition."

Parker and her people aren't conversational types. They've already huddled in one corner of the room, muttering to each other over the opened clue. Brad is dialing up someone on his phone—does he really think there's an expert on call who can decipher our grandfather's brain?

Hallie gives me an inquisitive look. "Well, he sure knows how to spice up a party," she quips. I laugh.

"Come on." I sling my arm around her waist. The combination of soft silk and warm skin underneath is almost enough to distract me from my grandfather's shenanigans. "Let's leave them to fight over the scraps."

I steer her out onto the terrace that overlooks the ocean. A salty breeze washes over us. Through the window, I can see the rest of my family still running around like someone, well, threatened to cut off their lavish lifestyles.

"I knew he was up to something," I say, amused. "And look at them. If you ever needed proof that there's nothing my family loves more than money . . ."

Hallie takes the envelope from me. "So are you going to open it or what? I'm dying of curiosity here."

I tuck it in my pocket. "And get caught up in that chaos? Yeah, I'll take a pass. How about we go find another drink?"

I make to head back to the party, but Hallie is staring at me in disbelief. "You're not even going to look? It's your whole inheritance on the line!"

"They can keep it," I shrug.

"Says the guy who's never had his rent check bounce." Hallie sounds skeptical. "Trust me, once you're broke with us mere mortals, you'll be wishing you fought a little harder for the throne."

"I'm not going broke any time soon," I reassure her. "I make a decent salary, and I've been lucky with some investments over the years. Believe it or not, I don't live like this all the time." I nod to the fresh lilies tied to every railing, and the lavish lights twinkling all the way down to the dock. "I'll be just fine."

"But . . . but . . ." Hallie stammers, looking so flustered it's hard not to kiss the words right off her lips. All night, she's been tempting me in that incredible dress of hers, the silk pouring off every delectable curve. "This is the Carlisle company we're talking about."

"And I don't have to get sucked in. The last thing I want is to end up stuck in an office all day. If they want the company, they can have it."

"Really?" Hallie folds her arms over her chest. I manage not to stare at the amazing things that positioning does to her cleavage. "You don't care about Carlisle Publishing *at all*? You don't even like the rest of your family—what do you think they're going to do with the company if one of them wins?"

I pause, reluctant. "They'll probably sell it off. They've been waiting for the chance for years."

She raises an eyebrow at me. "And that doesn't bother you?"

"Yes," I admit. "But if Grandpa has made his mind up to give it all away, then there's not much I can do about that."

"You could at least *look* at the first clue," Hallie says, plucking it out of my pocket. "The curiosity is killing me!"

"OK, OK." I smile at her expression. She rips it open and pulls out a piece of heavy cream cardstock with neat black print.

"*My love runs on a heart of gasoline,*" she reads aloud. "*Break it open for the next clue to be seen.*" Hallie looks at me, confused. "What does it mean?"

Despite myself, my mind races ahead. Already I'm picturing the cherry-red Camaro parked in its place of honor in Gramps's garage. "It's a car. *The* car."

He loves all his vehicles, but that one—that one he always told me was special. I can remember him stroking the hood and calling her darling. "I wouldn't be surprised if he loved it more than my grandmother. He spent hours tinkering with it in the garage . . . Which must be where the next clue is."

"So? What are we waiting for?"

I pause. I said I wasn't going to get sucked into this harebrained treasure hunt. But I was the only one who spent all those hours in the garage with him. The rest of the family might be able to figure out he's talking about a car, but they won't know which one.

Damn.

"It wouldn't hurt just to *look* at the next clue," Hallie adds. "I mean, at least it would slow the rest of them down."

"Good point." I can't think which one of those vultures I would want to win. Flora, maybe? But I do know Artie and Parker will be out for blood. "Come on."

I take her hand and lead her down the terrace steps and across the lawn, taking a shortcut around to the garage. The place is empty when I click on the lights.

"Nobody else has figured out the clue," Hallie says.

"Yet."

Instead of going straight to the Camaro, I duck into the side room and grab a toolbox. The clue said to break open the heart. He must want someone to take apart the engine, and you better believe I'm going to do it the right way.

Hallie follows me over to the Camaro. "Wow!" she says when she sees it. "That's a beauty."

"My grandfather sure thinks so." I pop the hood. All right, time to get down to work. I rub my hands together, feeling a spark of excitement. Crazy family dynamics aside, I can't help but warm to the challenge.

"See, I knew you'd get into the spirit," Hallie says, noticing my smile.

"What can I say?" I grin. "There's nothing like the thrill of the chase."

"Right." Hallie's voice flattens, but I don't have time to wonder what she means. I turn my attention to the engine instead.

You can't rush a disassembly job. First task: draining the fluids.

"Is there anything I can do?" Hallie asks.

"Grab that bucket over there?" I ask, pointing. "Otherwise . . . Keep our competition distracted if they catch up."

"I think I'm up to that."

I've finished the coolant and started on the oil when my cousins finally burst in. "Of course it'd be *here*," Artie says, sounding disgusted. "And look who's already got a head start."

Parker and Brad barge in right behind him. The Crossfit Kings look around with a huff. "What are you doing over there, Max?" Parker demands, drill-sergeant style.

"Me?" I ask innocently. "I just needed a break from the party. What are you all doing here?"

"Very funny." Artie scowls. "You expect us to believe you're not playing, too? You just felt like coming out here and leaving your fiancée high and dry."

"Oh, no," Hallie says demurely, leaning against the side of the car in a way that shows off her curves in that dress to full effect. "Not high here, and definitely not dry. There's nothing much more appealing than a man who knows his way around an engine."

I nearly drop my wrench. Why am I putting my hands to work on this car instead of that body again?

Artie looks like he's momentarily choked on his tongue. Cordelia glares daggers at Hallie and grasps her husband's elbow. "Forget them. He's making a guess. We've got the whole rest of the garage to search."

"Not if we get there first," Parker snaps. "Come on, Brad."

They rush into the maintenance room. Clangs and thumps echo out as they paw through Gramps's supplies. Artie leaps to the nearest car and yanks open the trunk. The hood. Each of the doors, peering inside. It's a frantic rhythm of *sigh*-slam!-*sigh*-slam!

Hallie leans in. "Are you sure you have the right car?" she whispers.

I nod. "Let them tire themselves out. I know I'm in the right spot." I remove the cylinder heads and get started on the nuts and bolts.

"Then I better go get started on that whole distraction part." Hallie glides away.

I'm too focused on the engine to watch her go, but I hear what she's up to soon enough. The clattering and slamming is briefly broken by a squeal.

"Oh, I'm *so* sorry, did I tip that oil can over on your dress?" Hallie exclaims.

"Leave it!" Cordelia says. She's gnashing her teeth over there now.

Parker and Brad have given up on the maintenance room and are now tossing all the cars at the other end of the garage in a flurry.

Hallie ambles over that way. "Did you find anything yet? Oh, did you remember to look under the seats? That's always where I lose stuff. Hey, I'm just trying to help!"

I smile. I ease open the engine's main casing—and bingo. There's another linen envelope, sealed in plastic, waiting inside.

I try to slip it out of the engine as surreptitiously as possible, but Artie has the eyes of a hawk. A gold-digging, entitled hawk.

"Max has it!" he yells, hurrying. "Give it to me."

He holds his hand out. I stare back. "Yeah, I don't think so. The clue is mine."

Suddenly I'm surrounded by a full set of cousins and spouses. Parker stomps closer, her hands fisted at her sides. "Look, Max, if there's only one clue, we all need to know what it says."

I raise my eyebrows at her. "And what are you going to do if I say no? Beat me up?"

She looks like she's considering it. Brad cracks his knuckles and tries to loom over me, although that's tricky given that we're the same height.

Hallie squeezes past the others to join me. "Max found it fair and square," she argues. "Or are the rest of you cheats?"

Artie's face flushes. "Don't you *dare* call me a cheat," he says, jabbing a finger at her. For a second I think he's going to be the one to start the brawl.

My exhilaration is fading. I didn't even want to be *in* this competition.

"Whatever," I sigh. "Don't start a riot. I'll read it out loud so you can all hear."

"And show us, too," Cordelia demands. Her satin dress is stained with oil, and her fancy hairstyle is coming loose. "In case you lie."

I bite back a retort. The sooner they get the next clue, the sooner they'll be racing off to solve it—far away from me.

It's another card, blank white with elegant black lettering.

"*Know your history if the others you want to best,*" I read out. "*Journey to where the great Walter Carlisle laid his head to rest.*"

I flip the card around so they can all snap photos of the text.

"Where he laid his head to rest . . ." Arties says thoughtfully. "Great-great-grandfather Carlisle lived in Boston when he first arrived in America, while he was building the business."

"That's it!" Parker barks, yanking Brad toward the door. "Let's go."

They all take off, leaving Hallie and I alone.

"So, about that drink?" I arch an eyebrow at her. "Plus, I think I need a dance with my new fiancée. You know, to really sell the act."

And getting to hold her close has nothing to do with it, of course.

But Hallie is just gaping at me, looking frustrated. "They're getting away!"

"Yup. Far, far away, I hope."

I lock up behind us, and stroll back towards the party—until Hallie grabs my hand, yanking me to a stop. "Why did you solve the first clue, if you were just going to quit the race?" she asks.

"I didn't quit."

She arches an eyebrow at me. "So you're fine just walking away?"

I shift, uncomfortable. The truth is, I don't want Artie, or Parker, or any of them taking over the company. And it *was* pretty fun, chasing down that clue . . .

"Yes," I lie. "I'm fine. This place will be a whole lot more relaxing with them off on some wild treasure hunt. More time by the pool for us," I say. "In fact, that sounds like a great plan. Fancy a dip?"

I tug her in the other direction, down towards the pool. It's glowing in the dark, illuminated by hundreds of underwater lights, and with everyone inside at the party, we're totally alone. "No trunks, but what's a little skinny-dipping between friends?" I wink.

"You first," Hallie says, with the strangest expression on her face. But hey, I don't need another invitation, not when the temperature is soaring between us. It's been almost twenty-four hours since that steamy kiss between us. Twenty-four hours far too long.

I strip off my tux, leaving my briefs on for the sake of her modesty, and dive into the pool.

Ah, that's better. "The water's great," I call, splashing lazily. "Come on in!"

But Hallie kicks off her shoes and sits on the edge of the pool, rifling through my pockets for . . . the second clue.

"Come on," I call. "I told you, leave them to it."

She scans it, looking thoughtful. "You know," she starts, and then shakes her head. "Maybe it's nothing."

I roll onto my back, floating. "What?"

"It's just—are you completely sure Artie was right about going to Boston? I'm just thinking about the phrasing. *Where he laid his head to rest.* When people talk about laying someone to rest, they usually mean *burying* them, not sleeping."

Huh. Now that she mentions it, that's true.

"And I figure your grandfather chose his words very carefully," she adds.

I swim over to her. "You think it means his grave, not his first home."

"If the others hadn't said anything, that's what I would have guessed," Hallie says. "Is he buried in Boston too?"

"No," I reply, thoughtful now. "He ended up retiring in a little town in Virginia. Harperville. That's where the grave is. Gramps took us all out there one time when we were kids."

"So everyone else is heading in the wrong direction." Hallie's eyes sparkle in the dark. "Which means we could get a head start and beat them all to the next clue."

"Or be chasing our tails for nothing," I point out, tugging her bare ankle.

She kicks back, splashing me playfully. "I thought you loved the chase."

"When it's a pretty woman, sure. When it's my family legacy, not so much."

"But don't you want to see Artie's face when you beat him?" Hallie asks with a mischievous smile. "And Parker would lose it. Completely."

I laugh at the thought. "Tempting . . ."

"So?"

Hallie waits for my response, and just like that, I decide. But it's not the thought of besting my cousins that makes me change my mind, or the prospect of winning control of the Carlisle Empire.

No, it's the flush of excitement on Hallie's face. The sexy-as-hell look that says behind Ms. Professional's trusty notebook and ground rules, there's a woman who loves adventure.

And damn, if I don't want to show her a wild ride.

"OK, you've convinced me," I grin, pulling myself out of the pool. "Let's go win this thing."

12

HALLIE

"SO THIS IS how the other half live," I say, sinking deeper into the uber-comfy plane seat. How is it possible that this jet is cozier than any living room I've ever been in?

Across from me, Max grins. "Did I forget to mention we have a small private jet on hand? My bad."

"Small?" I repeat, gazing around the luxurious cabin.

"The cousins took the big one."

He offers me a glass of wine, and I take it, savoring the taste before I grab another of the fancy crackers that were also stored in the sideboard. "I'm surprised you don't have any caviar on board. What kind of ramshackle operation are you running here?"

Max grins. "Cute outfit," he notes, looking me over with a sizzling stare. "You should have worn it to the party."

I laugh. I'm wearing plain cutoffs and a tank top. I barely had time to change out of my gown and throw a few things back in my suitcase before we raced to the airfield. "I figured I'd better go practical," I tell him. "Who knows what other tricks your grandfather has up his sleeve?"

"Don't remind me." Max stretches out his legs next to mine. His ankle comes to rest against my bare calf. I can't bring myself to move away. What's a little footsy between friends?

"So I have a question for you," I say, trying to distract myself from the lean lines of his muscular body, still dressed in that tux. "If everyone else in the Carlisle family is . . . well, a piece of work, how did you make it out with some good still left in you?"

"Some?" he teases, nudging my ankle.

I try to give him a withering stare. "I'm withholding judgment. But based on first impressions, you're not a vicious piranha like the rest of them."

"My babydoll, she's so sweet to me," Max teases, and I laugh.

"That's right, pookie."

Max's expression turns thoughtful. "I don't know why I'm so different. Even growing up, I could never really connect with them. It felt like we were all playing a part, you know? Artie striving to be this cut-throat business tycoon to impress everyone, Parker fighting for attention by dominating every sport she could. My parents would stash me with family every summer, but I steered clear. I was busy getting in trouble of my own." He winks, and I don't have to ask to know that the trouble in question probably involved girls.

"What about you?" he asks. "You're taking all this in stride. Maybe insanity runs in your family too?"

"Is there any family that's completely sane?" I counter. "I guess mine is pretty normal, all things told. Mom and Dad have a house in the country, out in Vermont. All quiet and picturesque. Which of course drove *me* crazy when I was a teenager, because the last thing I wanted was quiet, but I survived."

"Clearly," Max says.

"My brother's in theater," I add. "He's a big-time Broadway producer, but he's about as grounded as any show-business person I've met." I shrug. "Maybe the Gages are just kind of boring."

Max snorts with laughter. "Hallie, the last thing you are is boring."

I flush, surprised at the compliment. "I guess I have been keeping you on your toes."

"Me and the rest of the family. Talking back to the investors. Revamping Cordelia's fashion choices," Max counts them off.

"Hey, you asked me to distract her."

"And now you're probably top of her hit list." Max grins over at me. "Don't worry, darling, I'll protect you."

"From Cordelia? I could snap her like a twig." I giggle and take another sip of wine. "It's Artie I'm worried about. He looks like one of those *American Psycho* guys—wound so tight, he'll explode."

"As long as we're a thousand miles away . . ." Max clinks his glass to mine in a toast. "Here's to beating them at their own game."

WE TOUCH down at a private airstrip, out in the middle of nowhere. Being Max, of course, he's arranged to have a rental car waiting for us, despite the fact it's the middle of the night.

"Next stop, the cemetery," he announces, getting behind the wheel.

"Are you sure you're going to be able to find it?" I ask, peering through the windshield. It's pitch black out, our headlights the only illumination for miles around.

"Siri never lets me down."

"Can Siri rush deliver some holy water and stakes?" I shiver as we pass an abandoned old barn. "Because it's like the first act of a horror movie out here."

"No stakes," Max says. "But I do have an excellent roundhouse kick."

"I guess that'll have to do."

He reaches over to pat my knee, and even though it's a casual gesture, barely touching for a moment, I feel the heat everywhere. "Don't worry," Max says with a grin. "I'll fend off the undead for you, any day."

"Good. Because I watched as much *Buffy* as the next girl, but vampires are definitely beyond the scope of our contract."

By the time Max pulls over at the small cemetery, rain is spitting from the dark night's sky. "I don't suppose you packed an umbrella?" I ask.

"Sorry. You can stay here if you want."

"Are you kidding?" I reach for the car door. "I want to see if we're right!"

I take two steps out of the car—and fall flat on my butt. SQUELCH. Max laughs, and then has to grab hold of the car for balance when he hits the mud patch.

"Here." He helps me up, and then strips off his jacket, settling it around my shoulders.

"I guess flip-flops aren't the best choice for a midnight stroll through the graveyard," I say, levering them out of the mud. "Let's find that grave and get out of here."

We search the gravestones, using our cellphones as flashlights in the dark. Distant thunder warbles. Max starts whistling a jaunty tune, as if we're out for a pleasant turn around the park and not creeping around in a graveyard. I raise my eyebrows at him.

"To scare away the vampires," he says innocently.

"I don't think I've ever heard of that trick before."

"Oh, yeah. It's a secret only known to the innermost circle of— Hey, I've found it!"

He points to a massive tombstone topped with an angelic statue. Even in the dim light, I can see the envelope clutched in the angel's hand.

"Yes!" I cry. "We were right!"

"*You* were right," Max corrects me. He grabs me by the waist and swings me around. "We did it!"

His victory is infectious, and I laugh, suddenly weightless. "Watch it!" I warn him. "The mud!"

Max sets me down gently, and brushes a strand of wet hair from my face. His eyes are stormy blue in the darkness, and his fingertips hot against my face.

My breath catches. My eyes drift to his mouth, and then just like that, he's pulling me close again, into a hot, reckless kiss.

Ahhh.

God, I've been dying to taste him again. His mouth is hard and possessive, claiming mine, and a shudder of lust rolls through me at the feel of him. His hands are all over me, molding me against him as the fire between us blazes hotter, and I forget everything. Like my rules, and our arrangement, and the fact I've sworn off men like him . . . None of it matters, not with Max's tongue doing wicked things to mine, and his body so hard against me.

Very hard.

Hello.

Max releases me, looking bashful. "I, uh . . ."

"That's one way to say thank you," I blurt, trying to keep things light.

He relaxes, running his hand through his tawny hair. The rain has left it roguishly rumpled again. His gaze drops to my mouth as if he's thinking of planting another one on me, and I'm tempted to beat him to it. But out of his embrace, I'm getting soaked—and cold. "We should, umm, the clue . . ." I manage, still flustered.

"Right." Max reaches up to grab the envelope. We huddle in the shelter of a nearby tree to squint at the words on the card.

Our fortune is built on words, and the words were built here/
Pressed into paper to be read far and near

"Is he talking about the publishing business?" I ask. "*The words were built here?*"

Max pauses. "Maybe he means the place where the first Carlisle newspaper got off the ground. Harperville. That's where it all start-ed." He pulls out his phone, and a few clicks later, nods. "It's just a few hours' drive from here."

I can't help but let out a yawn. He glances over. "Tired?"

"No," I lie. Then I yawn again. He laughs.

"You're right, it's been a long day."

"A long couple of days." I think back. New York, to Palm Beach, to Virginia . . . in less than forty-eight hours. No wonder I feel like I could curl up right here and sleep.

"The clue can wait until morning." Max takes a photo, and tucks it back in its hiding place. "Let's see if we can find someplace to sleep for the night."

We squish back down the muddy path to the waiting car. I can't imagine Artie and Parker having to clamber through all the muck—if they ever make it out here. "I wonder if they're all still racing around Boston."

"Here's hoping," Max agrees.

Back in the car, Max turns the heater on full-blast, and I snuggle deeper in his jacket. There's something cozy and intimate about wearing a guy's clothes. From the look he gives me before he starts the ignition, I have the feeling he's thinking the same thing. Well, maybe not the cozy part. The heat in his eyes practically ignites *me*.

Can we get back to the kissing part of this adventure again?

Down, girl. My voice of reason pipes up, reminding me of all the reasons we're supposed to stay platonic. Still, as the miles drift past, I can't help sinking deeper into this quiet, sensual haze we're in, with just the noise of the rain on the windscreen, and Max's steady breath, beside me at the wheel, making me imagine just what I would do if there were no stakes here, no contracts or consequences . . .

Suddenly, Max wrenches the wheel, jolting me awake. Before I can even say a word, I see a shape looming on the road right in front of us.

A deer.

Max slams on the brakes. The car swerves, and my heart lurches into my throat. We hit the side of the highway hard, then bump over the incline—and straight down, into a ditch.

13

HALLIE

"HALLIE? ARE YOU OK?"

Max's voice is panicked. I groan, and then stretch, testing my limbs, my neck. Aside from the pain where my seatbelt is cutting into my chest, I'm fine.

"It's all good," I manage. The only part out of whack is my heart thumping away at five times its usual speed.

I drag in a deep breath. "Did we miss the deer?"

"I think so."

"Well, at least we don't have to deal with Bambi's untimely death on our conscience." I start to laugh, as much out of shock as anything. "This day just wasn't exciting enough. You had to throw a car crash into the mix."

Max exhales, then chuckles. "Believe me, I'm done with excitement now. Give me a nice, boring, warm bed."

"And a cup of cocoa," I agree.

I ease open the door and step out. The whole front half of the car is tipped into the ditch, its rear up in the air. Max braces his hands against the hood and shoves, but I'm not at all surprised when it doesn't budge. He pulls out his cellphone, then grimaces. "And of course there's no reception in the backwoods of Virginia."

I look around, but the road is empty. "So what do we do now?"

"Now, we walk," Max sighs.

I glance up and down the dreary road. The rain has faded to a drizzle, but it's still spitting on my face. "Walk to *where*?"

"There's a town farther down this road. And maybe someone will come by who'll let us hitch a ride."

I look at him in his tux and me in my cutoffs, and have to laugh again. "Good thing we dressed for a hike."

We grab our bags out of the back and set off down the road. I figure we'll be walking for hours before someone comes along, but it's only ten minutes before the sound of an engine arrives. "Score!" I exclaim, turning to look for the car.

Except it's not a car. It's a massive eighteen-wheeler truck, fender rusty and hood dented, rumbling up the road like a prowling monster.

Max waves it down, and the truck pulls to a stop beside us. The driver shoves the door open and narrows his eyes at us.

If this were a horror movie, this is the part where we'd get chopped up by the homicidal lumberjack.

"Need a ride?" the trucker-lumberjack asks in a friendly voice.

I think I might prefer walking, but Max apparently knows no fear. "That'd be great, if you've got room," Max says. "Just into town. We had a little encounter with a deer." He waves toward the crashed car.

The guy nods as if this is par for the course out here in the Virginia wilds. Which maybe it is. "Squeeze on in, then. It's about half an hour down the road."

To my relief, Max gets in first, so it won't be me squished right up against the giant. As I clamber in after him, the trucker twists to offer his hand. "I'm Carl, by the way."

His half-buttoned lumberjack shirt falls open over a T-shirt that's . . . pastel pink. And sparkly. A couple of winged horses are frolicking across the chest.

"Um, hi, Carl. I'm Hallie," I say. I can't help staring at the shirt. Carl glances down and chuckles.

"I've got a five-year-old daughter back home," he says. "HUGE *My Little Pony* fanatic. She insisted we get father-daughter T-shirts."

Okay, maybe he's not a terrifying serial killer after all.

Carl plays the *My Little Pony* soundtrack for us all the way into town. "I know it's a kids show," he says, "but some of the lyrics are actually really deep."

Max and I exchange a look, and I try not to laugh.

Five songs later—complete with sing-along from Carl—I'm just about ready to howl. Luckily, we pull into a parking lot at a bar with a run-down motel next door.

"This is your best bet to crash for the night around here," Carl says, waving goodbye. "Safe travels tomorrow to you. And don't forget that friendship is magic."

The truck pulls away, and finally, I can let out the laughter I've been holding back for forty miles. "My little ponies?" I snort, shaking.

"Friendship is magic!" Max howls.

Finally, my hysterics fade, and I can take in the run-down, puke-green lobby of the motel. "Um, Max? Did we take a detour to the Bates Motel?"

He turns. "Drink first?"

"Yes, please."

We head to the bar, instead. Inside, it's divey as hell—but warm and dry. The lighting casts an amber glow over the beat-up wooden tables, and the whole place smells like beer and peanuts. But I'm hungry enough that even the peanut smell gets my mouth watering.

The bartender gives our clothes an amused look. "Take a wrong turn, did you?"

"Something like that," Max agrees. We order burgers and extra fries, and a couple of beers, and settle in at a corner booth. For the first few minutes, all I can do is inhale charred beef and toasted bun. It's actually one of the best hamburgers I've ever had. One point to Wherever The Hell We Are, Virginia.

When I come up for air, Max is grinning at me. "What? A girl's gotta eat."

"And you do know how to eat," he says teasingly. "Don't worry. I like a woman who isn't afraid to satisfy herself."

My eyebrows jump higher. "Interesting. Most men are intimidated by that. You know, afraid of not measuring up."

Max's grin grows. "I like a challenge."

I flush. Suddenly all I want to do is grab him and haul him next door to that sketchy motel. As long as the door locks, I'm good.

I look around, trying to ignore the heat pooling low in my belly. My eyes land on the pool table across the bar. "Want to play?" I blurt. "Pool, I mean," I add quickly.

"Is that a challenge?" Max looks amused.

"Take it any way you want."

And take me, too. Ahem.

We head across the room, and I shrug off Max's jacket. When I turn around, Max's eyes linger on my neckline for a moment before jerking back to my face. He reaches for a pool cue, the muscles in his arms flexing against his dress shirt.

Okay, forget hot. I'm outright scorching now.

I know I should call it a night before things get out of control, but that itch of curiosity is burning and I don't want to back off yet. Every moment with Max has turned into a madcap adventure, the kind I'll probably never have again.

I want him. He's made it pretty damn clear he wants me. And way out here in the middle of nowhere, nobody has to know if maybe, just maybe, we let things go a little too far . . .

I reach for a pool cue, sliding my fingers up and down its length. "Cue up?"

"My pleasure," Max says in a voice that sends a shiver up my spine.

I lean low over the table when I take my first shot. Lower than I really need to, let's be honest. Even a modest tank top can show off plenty of cleavage if you know how to work it right.

"Clean break." Max sounds impressed. "You've played before."

"Just a little," I lie. I hustled my way through college, but he doesn't have to know. Yet.

Max approaches the table, rolling up his cuffs over his lean forearms and unbuttoning the top two buttons of his shirt. I'm not sure I've ever found anything more tempting than that V of sculpted tan chest.

Then he sinks three balls in quick succession, and I realize I need to pay attention to the table if I don't want to crash out of this game.

I'm trying to line up a tricky shot when Max comes up beside me. He sets a hand on my waist, its heat seeping through the cotton, and leans close.

"Let me help you out with this one."

I want to tell him I'm just fine on my own, thanks, but I want him to stay right there even more. "Please, go ahead."

He slides his hand up my side and adjusts the position of my arm. My breath catches in my throat. He lets his fingers rest there on my bare shoulder, his thumb tracing a blazing line over my skin. "The right position is so important."

"At least as much as the size of your stick?" I suggest sweetly.

He laughs. "Take the shot."

God, how can I concentrate with him so *there*? I inhale and line up the cue. I shift my hips a little to the left so my ass grazes the fly of Max's pants. This time it's his breath that catches. I smile and smack the ball.

It sinks cleanly into the pocket.

"You're a tough competitor," Max says as we straighten up. If there was a spark in his eyes earlier, it's spread into a full-out blaze.

"I play to win," I say, chalking up my tip of my stick. "And winner takes all."

"My kind of game."

I run the table until I miss a tough angle, and then Max takes over, until there are just a couple of stripes left on the table. A sensible player would attack them each in turn, but I should have guessed, nothing about Max Carlisle is sensible. He lines up a shot to sink both of the remaining balls in one—and misses by a millimeter. Leaving the table in the perfect arrangement for me. I sent my last balls slamming into the pockets and then give him a smile.

He laughs. "So, winner. What are you going to take?"

Damn, is he trying to turn me on? My gaze travels down his body. Lust flips my stomach. And maybe it's the pneumonia, or the three beers talking, or maybe it's just the sexual tension between us finally at a boiling point, but I don't care about the rules anymore.

"You," I answer, meeting his eyes. "I'm taking you, over to that motel for the night."

14

HALLIE

EVERY TIME I kiss Max Carlisle I think it can't get any better than this. Every time so far, I've been wrong. We burst through the door of the motel room, barely pausing for air long enough to slam it closed behind us. Luckily, they had a vacancy, and even luckier, the clerk on duty didn't bother making small talk, he just slid us a key, and pointed us down the hall to get down to business.

The business of tearing this man's clothes off, right this second.

I grasp the front of his shirt, yank him back to me, and Max crushes his mouth against mine.

Yes, yes, yes. This is exactly what I needed. I kiss him back with everything I've got, trailing my hands down his chest. Max groans, pressing his body against mine. His fingers skim my hip, the side of my chest. His tongue delves between my lips, and I sink into him, losing my mind.

I'm tired of waiting. I want to devour this man.

Max seems equally keen on devouring me. He angles his head to kiss me even more deeply, gripping my waist and pushing me back flush against the wall. And I'm flushed, all right, from head to toe. Burning up everywhere his body touches mine. I'm surprised my skin doesn't sizzle when he slips those hands up beneath my shirt. He hasn't even touched anywhere all that exciting yet, and I'm already whimpering into his mouth.

He tears away from my mouth and trails his lips down the side of my neck. I gasp at the contact. At the same time an annoying part of my brain pipes up right then with an unwanted PSA. I've been running around all night in the rain and the graveyard muck, and I haven't exactly had any time to freshen up.

I catch Max's hand as he reaches for the zipper on my shorts. "Bathroom?" I ask breathlessly.

He looks confused.

"Shower," I clarify, and his mouth spreads in a smile.

He leans close, nipping my earlobe. "I like the way you think."

"Oh, I'm all full of excellent ideas," I say, leading him to the tiny bathroom and turning the water on. I tap the front of his shirt. "This, for example, should really be on the floor. And everything else you're wearing while you're at it."

"As the lady desires," Max agrees. "Although it'll go faster if you help."

Fuck yes, as if I need to be asked. I start wrenching at the buttons as he untucks the hem. I've only gotten three open before he seems to think that's good enough and pulls it right off. Suddenly I'm faced with a chest so solidly sculpted it'd fit right in with those Greek relics in his family estate's garden.

Mine.

I run my hands over the planes of those muscles. They flex, his skin hot against my hands. Max pulls me into another kiss, one so long and passionate I pretty much forget what the hell I was doing. The hiss of falling water finally penetrates my mind.

Right. Shower. Getting naked. I'm still into that.

Max clearly is too. He strips off my clothes in record time, I should feel awkward and exposed, standing there in nothing but a strapless bra and panties. But the appreciation on his face is worth the pause.

"You are fucking beautiful."

I blush, grabbing the waist of his pants. "*You* are still wearing too much."

He dips his head to my shoulder, kissing the crook of my neck, then my collarbone. My breath catches. I fumble with his fly. I've just tugged his pants down when he unclasps the back of the bra. It falls away in the wake of the hot, wet slide of his mouth.

I moan as his lips close around my pebbled nipple. His tongue slicks over the tip of my breast and I grip his hair, my hips arching toward him of their own accord. He slides a hand lightly across the front of my panties, and I moan aloud from the touch.

More. I want more of him. *Everywhere.*

I reach lower, and Max makes a choked, wanting sound as my fingers close around the hard, thick length of him. Just touching him makes me so fucking wet. We stumble back into the shower stall, and the second we're under the steaming hot water, he pushes me against the wall. His mouth slides against mine even more hotly than before. His fingers trace every curve of my body, gliding over my skin. The slick friction is the most blissful torture I've ever felt. I clutch his shoulders, pulling him in for another kiss. His palms circle my nipples with teasing strokes and then drift lower. When he cups my sex, I can't help bucking against his hand.

"Fuck, Hallie," he groans, and I whimper, riding his hand.

I reach for him, and he kisses me hard, and then I lose track of everything. The bliss of him stroking between my legs. The slide of my hands over his pecs and abs. The thick, straining heat of his cock in my hands, pumping harder until his fingers thrust up inside me. "Max!" I cry aloud.

"Shhh." Max kisses my neck. "We don't want to wake the neighbors."

Sinking to his knees beneath the spray, he presses kisses down my stomach. I clench in eager anticipation. Just when I'm about to scream for him to put me out of my misery already, he licks over my clit.

I gasp, my hips rocking. Max swirls his tongue over me again and again. His fingers slip between my legs to trace my slit. My head tips back against the wall, my breath coming in pants. My legs have started to shake. But Max holds me in place with one firm hand as the other thrusts and beckons just right, teasing the edge of his teeth over my clit at the same time. A cry escapes my mouth. "Fuck, yes. Right there. Oh, God."

I think I feel him smile against me. But let's be real, I'm so far gone it's hard to pay attention to anything except the waves of pleasure coursing through my body.

Max hooks his fingers inside me, hitting the perfect spot. He laps my pussy with a rough stroke of his tongue, and I shatter. Trembling and clenching around his fingers, my eyes rolling back. For a second, all I can see is stars. The orgasm crashes over me in a torrent of bliss.

I'm gasping, still wobbly, when Max straightens up in front of me. Every inch of his hot, wet skin is pressed against mine. It's fucking heaven. But still not quite enough.

I reach for his cock. "I want you inside me,"

Max lets out a shaky breath. "Hell, yes."

He shuts off the water and grabs a couple of towels, pushing me back to the bed. I barely have a moment to catch my breath as he retrieves a condom from his wallet, and then, yes, he's bracing himself over me, his tawny hair damp and his eyelashes dark from the shower.

Damn, he looks good enough to eat.

Later.

I pull him down to cover me, every inch of his skin damp and hot and delicious.

Sliding his hand under my ass, he tips me up to meet him. The tip of his cock brushes over me and I gasp, trying to arch closer.

But Max doesn't let me rush. He eases into me one hard, thick inch at a time, until I'm moaning. His cock fills me with a heady burn. I rock against him, trailing my fingernails down his back, eager for more.

"There," I gasp. "Oh God, right there!"

He catches my mouth with another kiss, searing and hard. Then he starts to move, thrusting into me with steady strokes. Each one sends me higher on the rising wave of pleasure. Dear powers that be, who do I have to thank for setting me up with this sex god? We've barely gotten started, and he's already put every ex I have to shame.

I wrap my legs around his waist, and he plunges even deeper. His cock hits that sweet spot inside me. I clutch him harder, matching his rhythm as well as I can. He caresses my breasts, his breath hitching. "Hallie. Fuck. You're amazing."

"I feel amazing. *You* make me feel amazing. Max—oh!"

He thrusts deeper, and my body quivers beneath him. A spiral of pleasure radiates from the thrust of his cock through every muscle. I feel as if I could float away. But I stay right here, cresting higher until —fuck—I shatter around him with a scream and Max shudders into me, and we both fall breathless to the bed.

So much for staying professional. But fuck, if that's what breaking the rules feels like, sign me up for more.

15

HALLIE

I WAKE, sleepy, to find Max curled up in bed with me. For a moment, I tense, then it all comes rushing back.

The kissing. The shower. The mind-blowing orgasms.

Good morning.

Sunlight is streaming through the ratty curtains over the motel bedroom window. *Bright* morning sunlight. I rub my eyes and look around for a clock. How late did we sleep? It was pretty far into the night by the time we got around to doing any actual snoozing in this bed.

I finally spot the glowing red numbers beside the TV. Almost eleven. My heart lurches.

"Max!" I shake him.

Max mumbles something in incoherent protest. His hold tightens around me. Who'd have guessed Mr. International Playboy would be such a cuddler? Any other time I might enjoy it, but right now . . .

I shake harder. "Wake up! We've got clues to find, a treasure hunt to finish, a billion-dollar empire to win. Remember?"

"OK, OK. Max yawns, pushing back his rumpled hair. Fuck me if he doesn't look even more delectable. And as for his morning surprise, currently tenting the sheets . . .

He catches me looking and gives me a sly grin. "He says good morning, too."

"He?"

"Um, yes. My dick is all man—in case you hadn't noticed."

I have to laugh. Then I realize I'm currently naked—in the least flattering lighting in the history of the world. I snatch the sheet to cover myself.

"I thought we were past the modesty stage," Max says, leaning in and pressing a kiss to my shoulder. "I mean, we *are* engaged, after all."

I snort, and then I'm not capable of any sound at all, because he's claimed my lips with that delicious mouth. Well, maybe I manage an embarrassingly eager whimper. For a few seconds the world narrows down to the heat of his body and the sweep of his tongue over mine.

Then there's a hammering on the door. "Check-out was at ten!" a voice yells.

We look at each other. "What do you say?" Max asks, teasing a fingertip over my bare skin. "We could ditch the hunt and stay here all day. I bet I can find some treasure down here . . ." He tugs at the sheet, and I'm tempted to just roll back in bed with him.

But we've come this far, and I haven't braved a creepy cemetery and hiked through the rain just to leave the prize to Artie and co.

"Raincheck," I tell him reluctantly, climbing out of bed. "Besides, in the light of day, I'm not sure we want to spend any more time in this bed."

Max looks around the grimy motel room, and then grimaces. "Good point."

I scramble out from under the sheet and paw through the bag I brought. I know Max said to pack for every eventuality, but what outfit says "madcap billionaire treasure hunt"?

By the time I've freshened up, Max has already ordered a cab to take us into town. I look around, curious, as the open countryside makes way for a small-town main street—or what's left of one. A bank. A post office. A little corner store that's as close as a place this size gets to a grocery market. "This is it?" I ask. "It's hard to picture a Carlisle here."

"Back then, we kept things modest."

"Only one helipad?" I tease. Max chuckles.

"Take a left," he tells the driver. "There it is. The Carlisle building."

We pull up outside an imposing Victorian house that looks like it should have been producing witch's potions, not newspapers. I'm a little afraid the steps are going to crumble away under my feet.

"We don't do anything with this place anymore, but my grandfather holds on to it for sentimental reasons," Max tells me as a housekeeper lets us in. "If you can imagine Franklin Carlisle getting sentimental."

"I'll take your word for it." I peer around the large workroom beyond the front hall. The interior is clean, but the air smells kind of stale. It looks like nobody's touched the place in decades. "Okay, where do we start?"

"I guess just work our way from one end of the house to the other," Max says. "You take this floor, and I'll take upstairs?"

"Works for me." I brush my hands together and dive into the search. I peer under desks, rummage through drawers, and pore over shelves of boxes and stacks of paper. Franklin's making sure we *work* for this, isn't he?

I sneeze as I stir up some dust from one of the boxes. Nothing in there but some old printer templates. I glance around the room. Where is the actual printing press, anyway? Max's however-many-greats-grandfather couldn't have run much of a publishing business without one.

When I reach the far end of the ground floor, I poke at a sack leaning in the corner. A mouse darts out from behind it. I squeal, jumping about a foot in the air. Max is at my side in a second.

"No clue here," I say, pressing my hand against my chest over my racing heart. "And no big deal. Just a dumb mouse." I glance over at him, abruptly aware of how close he's standing and his fingers resting on the small of my back. "Thank you for racing over to my rescue, though."

"I told you. Protection from the undead—and small vermin." He smiles. Have the corners of his eyes always crinkled up adorably when he does that, and I just never noticed before?

Okay, Hallie, get a grip. I take a breath. "Any luck upstairs?"

"Nope. But I could get lucky down here . . ." Max tugs me closer, and leans in for a kiss—

Then the front door slams.

"All right!" Parker's voice barks. "Spread out. We've got to scour this place from top to bottom."

Shit. Max and I exchange a grimace. So much for our head start.

"Come on," I say, grabbing his hand. "They don't need to know we've already searched this whole place."

We creep down the hallway as they charge up the main staircase. I peer around the corner, and catch sight of a couple of guys I don't recognize, racing up after them. "Have they hired help for the search?" I whisper. "Isn't that cheating?"

"Franklin didn't exactly give us a rule book," Max points out.

The front door swings open again, this time with Cordelia and Artie. I guess they carpooled. Or private jet-pooled.

"You." Artie glares at us. "I suppose you knew all along Boston was a dead end?"

Max shrugs. "Is there a clue here? I'm just showing Hallie the old Carlisle haunts."

"Hurumph." Arties storms past us.

"What do you think?" Max asks, when we're alone in the hall-way. "Should we keep looking here? I don't think we missed anything."

"I don't know . . ." I glance at the musty photos framed on the wall behind him. There are old shots of the building, and framed newspapers, too. *Carlisle Press Donated to Local Museum,* one article headline reads.

"I'll do one last sweep," Max says. "See you outside in five?"

"Sure."

He heads up after the others, and my gaze goes back to the wall.

The printing press . . .

The last clue said something about where the words were "built" and "pressed into paper." Which could mean the building where it was done . . . or it could mean the machine that literally did the pressing. That would be just like Franklin, wouldn't it? Pick the one thing that's not in the actual building.

Footsteps thunder down the stairs. It's Brad, cellphone out, probably trying to get signal. "Can we get infra-red imaging?" he demands. "I'll upload the live-scans to home base."

He stops, seeing me there. Then a weird glint enters his eyes. "Hallie," he says, coming closer. "How's it going?"

"Just dandy," I reply, suspicious. "Crazy chase, huh?"

"Sure." Brad chortles. He looks around, and then lowers his voice. "You know, Parker and I were talking. You've got some smarts. We've got lots of cash. What would you say to becoming a double agent? Slip us some info, we slip you a couple hundred grand when this is over?"

Ugh. I don't want this dude slipping me anything, thank you very much.

"Thanks for the offer," I say brightly, "but I'm happy where I'm at right now."

Brad drops the smile. "We're going to win, you know," he says. "So, if you change your mind and want to be on the winning side . . ."

"I'll know where to find you," I say sweetly. "A day behind me and Max."

"What's that, *mon demi glace?*" Max rejoins us.

"Nothing, pookie bear." I take his hand. I'm itching to tell him my idea about the clue, but not in front of any of these bozos. "Come on, we should get going."

"Where?" Parker pops up, looking at us suspiciously. Suddenly, Artie is leaning over the bannister.

"Did you find something?" he demands. "What? Where?"

Dammit. They won't let us out of their sights. Unless . . .

"Come *on*, Max!" I make my voice as bratty as possible. "We've been trampling around this place *forever*, and you promised me you'd take me shopping."

Max looks weirded out by my sudden change in tone. *Go with it,* I try to telepathically communicate.

"Ugh. This place is *so* dusty," I continue, channeling a drama queen. "It's killing me with my allergies. I don't think I can stand being in here one more *second*."

"But there are still a couple rooms we haven't checked."

"I don't care about this stupid scavenger hunt anymore! My lungs are closing up here. I think I'm going to faint." I drape my arm across my forehead. "Don't you care about anything other than your stupid fortune? God, how can you be so *selfish*!"

I wink at Max. His mouth twitches.

"You go on out then," he says, warming up to the argument. "I've got to find this clue. Because yeah, it does matter a lot to me. You wouldn't understand."

I huff. "You always say things like that. We're supposed to be in this *together*. I can't believe I'm spending this vacation running around old buildings with my nose running like a faucet."

He throws his hands in the air. "Well, what do you want me to do about it?"

"You could come outside with me and take a walk. Since I *am* your fiancée. That should count for something. Or do I not matter at all?"

"Come on, Hallie, don't be like that."

"I can't help my allergies." I sniff. "And if you leave me on my own when I'm feeling this bad, you can take that ring back."

I flounce toward the door. Max groans and hurries after me. The other rooms have gotten a lot quieter all of a sudden. Yeah, we've got an audience all right.

"You'll be fine without me for a few more minutes," Max protests as we head outside.

"It's not about whether I'll be *fine*. I want to know I can count on you. And obviously I can't."

"Of course you can. It's just that this hunt—"

"Is totally and *completely* ridiculous!"

I march out the front door and slam it behind me. Max bursts out a moment later. "All right," he says, his voice mock-angry while his eyes dance with amusement. "Fine. But if I lose out because of your stupid allergies—"

"Don't talk to me like that!"

"Oh, come on, have your walk."

He takes my elbow, and I let him drag me down the block. When we're definitely out of hearing, he drops his voice to a whisper. "What was that all about?"

"I think I know where the clue is," I murmur. "Any idea how we get to the local museum? The actual printing press from the Carlisle building is there."

He laughs. "And the spoiled brat routine . . ."

"Was to throw them off the scent."

"You're a devious woman, Hallie Gage."

"Better believe it," I grin.

After all the theatrics, finding the museum is a piece of cake. It's just a few blocks away, and—

"Closed?" I groan in disappointment. I hadn't realized it was so late, but we spent the whole day searching the house, and it's after seven p.m.

"Until ten tomorrow morning," Max reads from the sign.

"But we can't wait that long!" I protest. "By tomorrow, the whole gang could have figured it out. We need to get in there now."

"What do you suggest?" Max asks.

"We could call the docent, and beg for admittance today?"

"That would just draw attention," Max says. "We want to stay under the radar."

"There's always breaking and entering," I joke. Max looks thoughtful. "I was kidding," I add quickly, but he just arches an eyebrow at me with a devilish look.

"It's hardy Fort Knox, just look at the place. And we would be guaranteed a massive lead over the others . . ."

I follow his gaze to the building, noticing the row of high windows, and—isn't one of them already open?

God help me, this man is a bad influence. Because I'm actually considering his crazy plan.

16

MAX

I WASN'T EXACTLY 100% serious about the whole "breaking in" thing, but one look at Hallie, her eyes lit up in anticipation, and I know there's no going back.

Damn does this woman look hot when she's ready for action.

"What do you say?" I grin. "Let's see how good your cat burglar skills are."

"You're a bad, bad influence, Maximillian Carlisle."

"That isn't a no."

Hallie shakes her head. "Well, if we're going to do this, we can't stand around casing the place," she says, ever the sensible one. Even when it comes to vaguely illegal activity. "This way."

We slink down the alley beside the museum building, out of sight from the street.

"I don't see any security cameras . . ." Hallie sounds relieved.

"Probably because nobody would be bored, or crazy, enough to try and steal a couple of old dioramas and an antique printing press." I check the row of narrow windows, set about six feet off the ground. "This is our best way in." I reach up and test the first window, then the next. Those two don't budge. But the third one, about halfway down the building, squeaks open at my nudge. I ease the pane as far up as I can. The room on the other side is dark. It's going to be a tight fit, but I didn't make it through reporting in five different war zones without developing a knack for getting out of tight spaces.

"Ladies first?" I offer.

"Right," Hallie says. "Just throw me into the line of fire ahead of you."

"I really hope no one's going to be firing on us in there," I say with a grin. "But if you want to try and boost me first . . ."

"Good point."

I offer her my cupped hands. She steps up and I heave her toward the window.

Hallie scrambles through the opening headfirst—giving me an excellent view of her shapely rear in those jeans.

"You better not be staring at my ass right now."

Can this woman read my mind?

"No comment," I reply, grinning.

"Hurumpg." She makes a noise, before hauling herself all the way through. There's the sound of a clatter, and then a thud.

"You OK?"

"Yup!" her reply comes. "But this miniature model of a farm . . . not so much."

I wince. "I'll leave a donation."

I grab the ledge and pull myself up after her, glad at least that all those pull-ups with my sadistic trainer were good for something. It's a tight squeeze through the narrow window, but I manage to wriggle through.

"Look out!"

Hallie's warning comes a moment too late. I drop heavily to the ground inside—and send us both tumbling to the floor.

"OOF."

We roll, until she's laying beneath me. Eyes bright, laughing smile, looking like temptation there in the darkness.

Fuck, this girl is beautiful.

I kiss her, hard, and Hallie responds immediately with a little noise that gets me hard in an instant. Her arms wrap around me, her fingers tracing over the back of my neck. A surge of lust bolts through me, and damn if I don't want to strip her naked and take her right here until she's screaming my name—

In the middle of the county museum. Where we just broke in.

OK, maybe not.

I pull back with a reluctant groan. Hallie sits up, her cheeks deliciously flushed. "I . . . guess we should find that clue?"

"And fast. Before I ravish you against this"—I check the label —"nineteenth century agriculture exhibit. Those folks knew how to throw down."

She laughs, and it's such a joyful sound, I can't even focus on anything else. How am I supposed to care about Gramps's ridiculous treasure hunt when I've got a woman who looks like that looking at me like that? But somehow when I offer my hand to help her off the floor, I don't immediately drag her back into my arms.

"Come on." Hallie looks around. "We need to be quick, before anyone comes."

"I disagree on principle," I joke, sliding my hand over her ass. "But OK."

She bats my hand away, giggling, and we start to search the museum. We find plenty of dioramas and antique coins, but no printing press. "No sign here," I say, disappointed. Then I hear it. The sound of footsteps, approaching from down the hall.

"Crapwaffle!" Hallie whisper-exclaims. "Who is that?"

I tug her through the nearest doorway and around one of the display cases showing off a great selection of what appear to be . . . doorknobs? Sure.

We squeeze into the space behind the case. Her breath spills hot against my neck, and I try to focus.

Possible arrest vs. taking her right here.

Fuck, I'm getting hard again.

The footsteps tap closer. A flashlight beam flicks through the room we're in. I peer around the case and make out the shape of a security guard, just some kid in an oversize uniform, with his headphones on.

As his footsteps fade away, I exhale in relief. Hallie sighs too, her chest rising and falling against mine, too luscious to resist.

I bend down and capture her mouth. Her lips part under mine, her tongue teasing mine in a sensual dance. I rock against her. She lets out a little moan, and then clamps her mouth shut, her eyes widening.

Right. Security guards and driving Hallie out of her mind with pleasure aren't going to be a good mix. Damn it.

"Come on," I whisper, checking that the coast is clear. "It's got to be down here, we've checked everywhere else."

When we get to the next doorway, Hallie clutches my hand tightly. She points. An old printing press is sitting against the far wall. And sticking out from one corner, I spot a linen envelope.

Victory!

Muffled voices reach my ears at the same moment. Shit, have my cousins picked up the trail? I grab the envelope, pull out the paper inside, and snap a picture of the clue with my phone in the light from the window. There's no time to read it right now.

Hallie slinks back to the doorway as I return the envelope to its hiding place—maybe tucking it a little farther in than it was when we got here. I don't have to be a perfect sportsman, right? There should be some advantage to getting here first. Then I join her by the hall.

Artie's voice is ringing out louder now. "We demand entry. An important piece of our family's property is located in this museum. It's imperative that we examine it right away."

Whoever he's yelling at says something in response that I can't make out.

"Now, look here," Artie starts up again.

Hallie whispers. "Well, I guess we're not going out the front door."

"Back the way we came?"

She nods, and we skulk back through to the room we came in through. This time, Hallie doesn't hesitate before taking my boost and climbing up to the window. She pokes her head outside. "The coast is clear. Here I go."

She's more confident the second time, just seems to slither right out with a quick gasp when she hits the ground. I pull myself up after her and—

Huh.

I push myself through to the waist, but I can't seem to maneuver myself the rest of the way through. I grit my teeth, squirming. Hallie's eyebrows leap up. "Are you *trapped* in there?" she says, sounding like she's holding back another giggle.

I glower at her. "Just give me a second."

Hallie's eyes suddenly widen. "Try harder! Someone's coming!"

I can hear footsteps approaching—outside, this time. Just down the alley . . .

Shit.

I shove at the ledge, trying to level myself through, but it's too tight.

Hallie pales. "They're getting closer!"

I can only imagine what will happen if someone finds us like this. "Sorry, officer, just some light criminal trespass, no hard feelings." And if the press get wind of it, and Franklin's madcap treasure hunt . . .

Let's just say my low profile won't last long.

Dammit!

Hallie reaches up and tries to yank me through. "You had to have extra fries," she hisses.

"Hey!" I protest. "There's not a spare ounce of fat on me."

"Tell that to the window."

She lets go, and looks wildly around. "Wait here," she orders me, then disappears around the side of the building.

As if I'm going anywhere in a hurry.

For a moment, I think she's gone and abandoned me to face the cruel arm of the law on my own. Then her voice carries back to me, sweet as sugar.

"Hi!" she exclaims loudly. "Do you work here at the museum?"

"Yes ma'am."

"Perfect. I have some questions, and you look like a man who has all the answers."

She's stalling. Yes! I should have known she'd have my back. Somehow, Hallie has been supporting me since the moment this weird adventure began. From scornful relatives, to small-town security. How did I manage without her?

I wriggle faster as the guy chuckles. "What do you want to know?"

"Let me show you. There was something I saw . . . I know the museum isn't open, but I'm just dying to find out more. I'm a local history buff, and I heard you have an amazing collection of reproduction farm equipment!"

Their voices fade as she leads him away—in the other direction.

Is there nothing this woman can't do?

I heave and yank and finally manage to haul myself free. This time there's no Hallie to break my fall. I hit the ground and stagger to my feet.

I guess you really can get *too many* muscles.

I'm brushing myself down when Hallie reappears. "Come on! He's gone to get me some pamphlets. Let's get out of here!"

We duck around the building before doubling back to the sidewalk. Parked out front are a couple of black sedans that stick out like sore thumbs.

"Your cousins' rides, I'm guessing." Hallie eyes them as I call up the taxi service. Her lips curl into another smile.

"You know," she says, "we could slow them down even more . . ."

"Uh oh. I'm getting to know that look," I tease. "It's your devious master plan kind of look."

Hallie glances around, but the street is empty. Just then, Artie's voice comes filtering out of the building.

"What do you mean, 'no'? I'll have your fucking job for this!"

"And there goes the last of my conscience," Hallie says. She leans over and unscrews one of the tire caps. Air starts hissing out.

I follow her lead. In a minute, all the tires are deflating.

"Hey!"

An angry cry sounds behind us. "What the fuck are you doing?"

Just in time, our cab pulls up. "Come on!" I grab Hallie, and pile her in the back. "Go! GO!" I yell to the driver, who's clearly been playing way too much GTA because he screeches away in a cloud of burning rubber.

"Come back!" Brad yells behind us, but they're too late.

We're already gone.

17

HALLIE

"A WINDOW TO THE WORLD. A *window* to the world. A window to the *world*."

I yawn. I don't really want to move any other part of my body. It's hard to want to do much of anything when I'm sprawled on the cushy king-sized bed in a fancy hotel room.

"You've been reading that clue for hours," I say. "It's not going to change this time."

Come to bed, I add silently. Ravish me all over again.

"*From inside and above,*" Max reads, "*it's a window to the world. Arrive to see it first, and you'll find your prize unfurled.*"

"Just when I thought your grandfather couldn't get any vaguer." I smile. "There's only about five hundred windows on this hotel building alone. Take the entire country into account, and, well . . . Plus, who says he's limiting this search to the *country*?"

If we start allowing for metaphorical windows, the whole thing gets even more impossible.

"I've still got nothing." Max sighs.

"But if we've got nothing, I can't see how Artie or Parker could have figured it out. Maybe you just need to sleep on it," I point out.

"And this is clearly the place to do it." I stretch out on the duvet, which is so soft it should be illegal. The suite is bigger than my apartment and ten times fancier. Marble sink and heated tiles in the bathroom, velvet furniture all through the main room—Olivia would love it here. I think that might even be actual gold in the wallpaper pattern. Because why not?

Max turns toward me, and if the heat in his expression is anything to go by, it's not *sleeping* he's thinking about right now. Before I can stoke those flames, his cellphone sounds. He glances at his phone and winces.

"It's my lawyers. I'd better see what they want."

Max heads into the living room—because yes, this is a whole fucking suite—and I snuggle deeper into the down pillows. This is the life. Gorgeous hotel room, check. Even more gorgeous man, double check.

Gorgeous diamond ring on my finger . . .

I gulp. Oh yeah, that whole "fake fiancée/contracted relationship" part of things. It had kind of slipped my mind, what with the crimes and misdemeanors—and wild, hot sex.

This definitely wasn't in the employee handbook.

I check my messages and see a couple of missed calls from Olivia. Whom I've been ignoring for days. Sure, I've been just a little busy on this treasure hunt, but also, my guilty conscience is waking from it's post-coital slumber. Sure, there wasn't anything in the contract forbidding consensual sex, but she spent so long stressing how professional her operation was, I'm guessing she wouldn't look too kindly on me blurring the lines like this.

I brace myself, and call.

Olivia answers on the second ring, her voice as smooth and warm as always. "Hallie! How have you been doing? I hope the radio silence means everything's going smoothly."

"Yes," I lie. "Just fine. Max's grandfather sprung a surprise on us, so we've been kind of busy."

I quickly fill her in on the scavenger hunt, and she laughs. "Wow. Well, I do tell my clients to expect the unexpected."

Like wild, hot sex in a gross hotel room. And barely escaping a minor felony with our limbs intact.

"Yup, it's been a ride!" I answer brightly. "Actually, I'm having fun. And Max . . . well, he's not what I expected."

Something must come across in my tone, because Olivia clears her throat. "Good, just as long as you remember this arrangement is temporary. I know it's your first time working like this, but it's easy to forget. Lines can get blurred, being in such close proximity . . ."

Is that her way of asking if we're banging like bunny rabbits?

I cough. "I remember. Lines, firmly in place."

"Good. I know it's easy to get swept up in the moment. After all, you're pretending to be in love. But at the end of the day, that's all it is. Pretend."

My face flushes. Thank God she can't see me. "Of course not. I know that."

"Great. Then I'll leave you to it. We can chat more when you're back in town. It's just another . . . three days."

"Right. Sure. See you then."

I hang up and flop back on the bed. Three more days? I can't believe it's flown by so fast. It doesn't feel like nearly enough time, not to get to know Max, and enjoy every last kiss . . .

Dammit.

I sit up, my stomach in knots. Olivia's right. I have let myself get swept away. Sure, I don't really believe Max and I are getting *married*. But I guess I was starting to think there might be something between us. A connection—besides the white-hot sexual chemistry, at least.

My heart sinks, and I try to look on the bright side. Maybe it's for the best that this thing has an expiration date. After all, I swore off playboys, and Max is about as playful as they come. I wanted a real relationship, didn't I? Sensible. Normal. Reliable.

After spending the past few days in a whirl of madcap desire, it sounds like I'm shopping for a vacuum cleaner.

Max emerges from the living room. "All set," he says with obvious relief. "Enough business for today. I'm ready to get on with the pleasure part of the evening. Room service?"

Spending the night here with Max—and food—sounds tempting.

Too tempting.

"How about we go out?" I suggest instead. "We've been racing around so fast, I've forgotten where we are. And what day it is."

"Your wish is my command."

Being Max, of course he already has the best restaurant in the city on speed dial, with the ability to finagle a last-minute reservation. And of course we end up at the best table in the place, by a big window that overlooks a scenic river. The lights sparkle off the rippling water and classical music drifts through the dining room. The tablecloths are so white I'm not sure it's safe to look straight at them, and the menu is just as lavish.

"What do you think, pookie bear?" I tease. "Foie gras before or after the truffles?"

Max laughs. "After, naturally. With caviar on the side."

I wrinkle my nose. "Does anyone actually like caviar, or is it just one of those things rich people eat to show off how cultured they are?"

"To tell the truth, I never could stomach the stuff," Max replies. "Give me a good old-fashioned steak any day."

"Sounds good to me!"

For the first few minutes after the food arrives, we're busy just filling our stomachs. Then Max leans back in his chair and pauses for breath.

"So, according to my lawyers, my cousins are all pitching a fit over this treasure hunt," he says, looking rueful. "Well, everyone except Flora. Apparently, they're still chasing their tails in Harperville. With eight flat tires."

I laugh. "I don't remember Franklin setting down any rules about fair play."

"If he had, they'd have broken them a dozen times over already." Max grins. "I have to admit, it's been pretty satisfying seeing them flailing around, always one step behind us. It's about time they realized they can't discount me just because I'm not around sucking up to the investors 24/7."

"Do you have any idea what your grandfather was thinking? I mean, I get that he's gone a bit, erm, batty, but this seems like a really crazy way to choose an heir."

Max shakes his head. "Honestly, I have no idea. I guess it's what he said about feeling like none of us is putting in the work . . . But this isn't exactly the kind of work it takes to run a corporate empire. Solving clues doesn't help all the hundreds of people the company employs."

"What would you do, anyway, if you win?" I ask. "I mean, not to jinx anything. But if the company is yours . . ."

"I don't know." Max pauses, his expression turning more thoughtful. "I don't want to give up traveling, but at the same time . . . Well, there could be some benefits to staying in one place. Putting down roots."

He meets my eyes, and my heart catches. Is he talking about us?

"I think you could do some pretty amazing things at the helm," I say shyly. "If you let them sell it off, who knows what will happen to the company—and all the employees?"

"Yeah." Max looks conflicted. "I guess I never thought about it like that. I figured the company would just keep on keeping on . . . But if they're serious about selling to the highest bidder . . . I wouldn't want to see the legacy we've built crumble, just like that."

I reach across and squeeze his hand. "Maybe it doesn't have to. I mean, how many more clues can there be? This time tomorrow, we could be at the finish line. And you could be the one deciding what happens to the company. You'd be a great CEO," I add loyally, and it's not just because I have a fantasy involving me, Max, and an executive desk.

He cares.

Sure, he can be reckless and charming, but I'm realizing that behind the playboy exterior, he's also thoughtful and concerned about his responsibilities. He's smart, and supportive, and—

Dammit.

These are real-girlfriend feelings. And a real girlfriend, I'm most definitely not.

"Anyway, I'm just saying, I hope for the company's sake, you win."

Max looks surprised. The intensity in his blue-gray eyes almost melts me. "You really mean that, don't you?"

I cough, embarrassed. "Compliments completely on the house. As cocky, reckless billionaire playboys go, you're not half bad."

The corner of his mouth quirks up. Oh, right, I forgot "devastatingly handsome." A phrase he's also totally earning right now.

"You know," he says, his voice dipping low, "in a lot of ways I'm glad my grandfather came up with this crazy scheme. It's made me rethink a lot of things I probably should have before. And it also brought you into my life. I should thank him just for that."

He squeezes my hand back. The warmth of his touch floods my entire body. I'm pretty sure I'm blushing. I want to ask him the questions I was asking myself just an hour ago. Is this real? Is he ever going to want to see me again after this week is finished? Could we actually build something like a relationship off the back of this mad adventure?

Luckily, Max interrupts me. "Now, what do you say we get dessert to go?"

MAX PRACTICALLY DRAGS me to the cab, and the second we're in the backseat, he pulls me hard against him in a smoldering kiss. God, he's already hard for me, and I can't help rocking against him, kissing wildly all the way back to the hotel. The elevator ride up to our room passes in a blur, and then—thank God—he's slamming the door shut behind us and pushing me up against it.

We're finally alone.

Max tugs down the straps of my dress to cup my breasts, and groans, his mouth leaving mine to mark a hot trail down the side of my neck. His thumbs brush over my nipples, and I whimper.

"Hallie," Max mutters against my skin. Every movement of his lips sends sparks shooting through me. "You drive me crazy. Can't stop thinking about you. And this." He pinches my nipples, making me moan. "And this." His hands drop to slide the dress the rest of the way up my thighs. His fingers trace the hem of my panties.

"If I can make a suggestion?" I say breathlessly. "Less thinking and more doing."

"Fuck yes."

We kiss again, so hard and hot my head is spinning. I ease my hands down his firm chest to the button of his pants. He shifts to give me better access as I wrench at that and then the zipper. In a matter of seconds, I've palmed his cock. "Fucking *yes*," he breaths, gripping my hips, urging me closer. I gasp as the hard length of him rubs against my clit.

"These need to go," Max says, hooking his fingers around the narrow band of my panties.

"Rip them right off," I murmur. "I've got more where they came from."

The heat in his eyes goes from sizzling to searing. With a yank, he snaps the fabric away from me, and then he's sinking to his knees, a wicked look in his eyes.

He licks over me in a hot swoop, and I sink back against the door, closing my eyes against everything except the feel of his mouth on me, and *fuck*, his fingers thrusting up inside.

Who the fuck cares how real this is? I wouldn't give it up for the world.

18

HALLIE

SOMEONE SHAKES MY SHOULDER. Someone evil, clearly, because I am *so* not ready to wake up yet. I mumble a scathing remark that would stop any villain in his tracks and press my face deeper into the pillow.

"Hallie," Max says, sounding both amused and impatient. "I need you up. I figured it out. The clue. I know where we're going."

"What? Where?"

He grins at me. "Gramps has a yacht called The Bird's Eye View. He sailed it all around the world when he was my age. A window to the world—that's got to be what he meant."

I rub my eyes and push myself upright. "Okay. So where is it?"

"Right back in Palm Beach. We're heading back to the start. Full circle—that's exactly the kind of poetic ending he'd like."

"All right," I say, managing to stifle a yawn. "I guess we'd better get a move on then."

He raises an eyebrow at me. "I did let you sleep as long as I could."

He's already dressed. Already showered, from the damp sheen of his hair. The fact that he let me sleep in is actually kind of sweet. I'd appreciate it more if I didn't want to fall back into the pillow—and drag me down with him.

But there's way more than just a mind-blowing orgasm on the line, and I wouldn't forgive myself if I was the one holding him back from the prize.

I heave myself out of the bed. As I reach for my bag, Max catches my shoulder. He touches my face to tip it toward his and gives me a kiss that's somehow soft and demanding at the same time.

"What was that for?" I ask, when we breathlessly come up for air.

He shrugs, and gives me a soft smile. "Just because."

I DOZE a little on the plane, enough that I'm feeling completely myself by the time we touch down back in Palm Beach.

"We won't have much time," Max says, looking worried. "The minute anyone sees us back here, they'll be on the phone to Artie and Parker. They have spies everywhere."

"So, we'll just have to be quick," I agree, squeezing his hand.

There's another car waiting on the tarmac for us, and it whisks us back to the estate in record time. Max leaps out the minute we pull up the driveway. "Come on!"

He grabs my hand, and I follow him through the estate's winding paths, down to the private dock. Sure enough, there are a couple of yachts moored, bobbing on the tide. Max makes a beeline for the biggest one.

"Is this a yacht or a cruise liner?" I exclaim, as we head up the gangplank. It's got to be a hundred and fifty feet, at least, with two levels of gleaming, polished decks. Max heads for the staircase, and I follow him down to—

"Holy shit."

Someone's transplanted an entire luxury bachelor pad into this boat. And by luxury, I mean white leather couches so soft my skin shivers when I touch them, full bar with marble countertop, an entertainment system with a TV bigger than my living room window back home . . .

And that's just the lounge area. Through another doorway there's a rosewood-paneled dining room with a ten-seater matching table and an honest-to-God crystal chandelier hanging from the ceiling.

Ladies and gentlemen, welcome to the lives of the rich-as-fuck.

The one thing the yacht is missing is a clue. Or a prize. Or whatever the hell that last clue was supposed to be leading us to. Max and I scour every inch of the place, opening cupboards and drawers, peering under the couches and the double-king-sized canopy bed. I ogle fifty-year-old wines and ornate gold candlesticks. But nothing looks remotely like an answer to this treasure hunt.

"It's got to be here!" Max exclaims, looking frustrated.

"We've looked everywhere."

"Then we look again!"

Finally, we tramp back out onto the deck. The teak lounge chairs with their plump cushions look perfect for relaxing, but neither of us is a mood to relax. I yank up the cushions to check under them, but no. Nada.

"I don't think it's here," I say to Max, disappointed.

He sighs. "No. I guess not. I was so sure . . ."

"The clue was really vague," I say. "You could still be right about the full circle thing. We just need to think about it some more. Maybe if we wander around the estate, something will click?"

"Yeah." Max runs his hand over his rumpled hair. "Might as well give it a shot. Let's split up to cover more ground."

"Oh." I try to hide my disappointment. What happened to us being in this together? "Sure, that makes sense."

Max heads for the house, and I wander the gardens. The hedge-sculpted famous figures look as if they're contemplating the problem too. The water in the pool is so still it reflects the clear blue sky like a mirror. I poke around the patio, thinking about windows. Views. A window to the world . . .

Yeah, I've still got nothing.

I hear a tapping sound and look up. Franklin himself is strolling on the verandah, his cane clicking on the polished ground. "Miss Gage," he calls. "I didn't know you were back."

"You mean, you thought the clues would send us somewhere else?" I frown.

He chuckles. "Ah, still playing my little game, are you?"

"Well, you didn't exactly give Max a choice," I point out. "Not if he doesn't want to see the company sold off to the highest bidder."

"Coming around then, is he?"

I'm not sure what he means. "Max has beat the others every step of the way, you know," I say. "He's been the first to every clue."

"I wouldn't have expected anything less," Franklin says enigmatically. His tone hasn't changed, but there's a twinkle in his eye. Suddenly I remember my conversation with Max last night, about how this hunt has really pushed only him out of his comfort zone. That first clue was set up perfectly for him, too, wasn't it? He was the only one who knew about his grandfather's favorite car, and knew how to take apart an engine.

If he hadn't gotten involved in the competition, the others would never have gotten past that first step.

I study Franklin's expression. "You want him to win, don't you? It's not really a competition. You're just testing him."

The old man's wizened face doesn't give anything away. "Now why would I do a thing like that?"

"For all you know, one of the others is going to cheat their way to the final prize," I say, frustrated. "And then you're stuck with them. Why don't you just sign it all over to Max? It would be a lot less trouble."

Franklin's eyes narrow. "That's the trouble with your generation. You think 'trouble' is a bad word. Trouble builds character. Trouble forces people to either roll over or step up. Until a person knows what he's made of, he isn't ready to take on any real responsibility."

Oh, not this bullshit again. "From what I've heard, Max has been running around reporting stories in war zones. I'm pretty sure he's already faced a hell of a lot more trouble than you're giving him here."

"There are different kinds of trouble," Franklin says lightly. "Adventuring doesn't prepare one to run a business." He looks me up and down. "Nor to settle down and put down roots. Marrying you will take him to where he needs to be, too."

Well, he's out of luck there, not that he needs to know that. "I don't know," I say. "It's your business, not mine. But I still think you're taking a pretty big risk here."

As if to put the proof to my words, an engine roars up the drive. Here comes the cavalry.

I head over to entrance to see what the cousins are up to. If they've figured something out, I'd like to hear it.

They're all pouring out of the car when I get there, Artie and Parker's crews together. I guess the sharks have officially teamed up now. Is there a word for that? A squad of sharks? A jerkishness of sharks?

"The maid said they only got in a few hours ago," Artie is saying as he strides to the door. "If they haven't found it yet, we've got time to catch up."

So they don't know anything, they're just following a tip. I step deeper into the garden before the cousins notice me.

My own search hasn't gotten me anywhere, so following the jerkish squad seems like a decent plan. Maybe they'll let something slip they don't even realize is important. They ought to know the family better than I do.

I slink along behind them into the house. Parker and Brad go barging into the kitchen wing with a clanging of pots and pans. They do like making a racket, don't they?

Artie and Cordelia take a different approach. Artie summons a few of the household staff and starts barking instructions about rooms to search. He and Cordelia start with the music room.

I putter around in the hall outside, checking behind the paintings on the walls, because why not? I wouldn't put anything past Franklin at this point. Artie's voice filters out of the room.

"He started this stupid hunt here. If the answer's anywhere in the house, it's probably in this room."

So he had the same thought as Max about Franklin going full circle. Any other brainstorms I could use? I edge toward the doorway.

"This is so ridiculous," Cordelia says with a huff. "I'm missing the Barnstone gala for this, you know."

"Cordy, if we win this, you can *buy* the fucking Barnstone Foundation. The prize has got to be somewhere. The old man might be insane, but he wouldn't send us on a chase without a finish line."

I touch the door, only meaning to lean a little closer. Unfortunately, I overestimate how stiff the hinges are and underestimate my lean. The door goes flying open, sending me stumbling inside. I catch myself, tugging my shirt straight and looking around wide-eyed as if I'm not sure how I ended up here.

"Excuse me, I was just looking for my purse."

Cordelia sneers. I guess she's been taking lessons from her husband. "You mean the purse that's over your shoulder?"

"Oh! Silly me. There it is." I give her a too-big smile and start to back out of the room.

"Hold on." Artie raises his hand and marches over. "How much do you figure Max is worth without the company?"

I blink, honestly startled this time. "Um, I don't know? And I don't really care."

"Let me tell you," Artie says slickly. "I make more in one day than he does in a month. You want to be set for life? Any information you get, you pass it on to us. I can see you never want for anything."

Funny, because what I really want is for this asshole to get out of my face. I stop myself just short of saying as much out loud. "Thanks, but no thanks," I say firmly. "I'm perfectly happy with the partnership I've already got. Good luck!"

He starts to sputter something, but I'm already walking away. This treasure hunt might be bringing out the best in Max, but it's getting to the worst in everyone else. The sooner it's over, the better.

19

HALLIE

WHAT DO you call a treasure hunt when nobody can find the treasure?

Boring.

It's two days since we all converged at the estate, and despite searching every square inch of the place, we've all got nothing. Bupkis. Nada.

"I'm missing something," Max says, pacing frustratedly. "There's got to be a piece I'm not fitting together."

I watch him, concerned now. It's past midnight, and I don't think the guy's had more than a couple of hours of sleep in days: there are dark shadows under his eyes, and his shoulders are hunched with tension.

"You need to get some sleep," I tell him. "Come at it with fresh eyes tomorrow."

"There isn't time." Max brushes off my concern. "You think Artie or Parker are sleeping?"

Probably not. They've kicked into high gear, too: bringing in guys in dark suits to prowl the grounds like FBI agents searching for evidence. This place is full of lawyers, threatening all kinds of suits against Franklin—who, of course, just smirks and ignores them—and I swear I almost tripped over a scientist with a lab coat and beaker out in the gardens yesterday. Don't ask me what the hell he was testing for.

A whole lot of effort, and no one has any prize to show for it.

Max slams his laptop shut in frustration. "It has to be here. Maybe he just picked a random spot and buried it in the lawn."

"Don't say that again," I warn him wryly. "Your cousins will have bulldozers out in the yard before sunrise. I'm kind of surprised they haven't started demolishing this place yet."

"Believe me, they would if they could." Max leans back in his seat, looking exhausted. "But this is all Grandpa's property—until the minute someone finds that final prize."

I glance out of the windows. They're flung open, the warm night breeze drifting in and moonlight glimmering off the ocean in the distance.

I take his hand. "Come with me."

Max leaps up. "Where? Did you think of something?"

"No. But you need a break."

"I can't."

"Yes, you can." I tug firmly. "You've been going around in circles for days. Clear your head, relax a little. Who knows, maybe it'll spark something?"

Max makes another noise of protest, but he doesn't resist. He follows me outside, and down the path towards the ocean.

"We've already checked the yacht. A dozen times."

"You've got a one-track mind, buddy," I say, as we reach the beach. It's a pale crescent in the moonlight, and I kick off my shoes, wriggling my feet in the warm sand. "But I bet I can make you forget all about the treasure hunt."

"Oh yeah?" Max doesn't look convinced. But that's before I strip my shirt off and wriggle out of my skirt. "What are you doing?"

"What does it look like?" I grin, stripped down to my underwear. "Skinny dipping."

"You can't skinny dip with clothes on." Max moves closer, his hands skimming over my bare waist. But he's not looking frustrated or bored anymore. No, that heat in his eyes is pure hunger.

"Then it's a good thing you're here to take them off me," I smile, flirty.

He chuckles. "If this is your idea of a distraction . . ."

I take my bra off.

" . . . it's an excellent one," Max finishes. He reaches for me, but I duck away.

"Race you!" I cry, and dash across the sand. I hit the water, splashing through the shallows, and then dive in. The water feels amazing against my bare skin, and I lie back, letting the salt buoy me up. There's a splashing noise, and then Max joins me. And yes, he's abiding by the rules of skinny dipping, too.

"Too slow!" I call, smiling.

"You had a head start."

He grins and kisses me, and I drink him in, sinking into the dance of our tongues and the stroke of his hands up my naked body. Heat surges through me. Everything he does feels so fucking good. I want to just drown myself in him.

I run my hands over the ridge of muscle in his shoulders, naked and wet from the tide. Max makes a low groan of pleasure and kisses me harder. He cups my breast, teasing his thumb over the peak until I whimper, and then his hand is sliding lower, between my legs.

I gasp. I can't believe we're doing this, out here for anyone to see. But the moon slips behind a cloud, and the water hides his slow, insistent stroking, and soon I'm whimpering his name over and over.

"Oh God, Max . . ."

He watches my face as his hand rocks against my core. Every pulse of his fingers sends me higher. The desire in his expression only makes me more giddy. He plunges deeper.

"Come for me, Hallie." He nips at my neck, his voice a low, commanding growl. "Come for me. Right now."

Who am I to resist such a sexy order? His thumb sweeps over my clit, and the water swells around our chests, and I break apart in his arms with a gasp.

Yes.

AFTER I COME BACK DOWN to earth, my fingertips are pruning in the water. Real sexy. "How about we take this to dry land?" I suggest, and we wade back to shore. We're just reaching the heap where we left our clothes when I hear voices carrying, and the swoop of flashlights.

"Someone's coming!" I panic. It's got to be one of the cousins or their crew, but the last thing I want is a family reunion while I'm naked and covered in post-coital flush.

"Quick, this way." Max grabs my hand, and I clutch my dress against my body, hopefully protecting my modesty as we dash through the shadows. Max skirts the main path, and yanks me to a low, sleek cabin set just back from the beach. We burst through the door, and Max eases it shut behind us. I peer out from behind the blinds.

"I don't think they saw us."

"Good."

His voice is right behind me, and then his hands are hot on my body. I turn, and Max kisses me until my head is spinning and the rest of my body is begging for more.

"What is this place?" I ask breathlessly, coming up for air. In the dim light I can make out a living area with couches, and some kind of bar . . .

"Beach cabana," Max answers, sounding distracted. His hands rove lower. "So you don't have to go back to the main house for a drink."

Of course. Any other time, I would marvel at the excess, but right now, I'm just thanking whatever moneybags designer came up with this bright idea. Because there's no way I can make it back to our bedroom, not with Max right here against me: naked, and wet, and so fucking perfect. I run my hands down his chest, reaching for his hard length. But Max captures my hands away.

"I'm not done with you yet."

He pushes me back on one of the soft couches and leans over me, dropping more hot kisses down my throat. His fingertips skim over my breasts with a torturously light touch that leaves me aching. Then his mouth closes over one nipple, the sweep of his tongue drawing it to a sharp peak in an instant. I moan, tangling my fingers in his hair, but it's still not enough. I slide my hand down his body and grip his cock. "I need you," I moan. "I need *all* of you."

"You've got me, sweetheart," he says. He finds a condom from his pants and rolls it on, pushing me back deeper into the cushions. I pull him down to cover me again, hungry to feel him, and then—yes—he's pressing into me inch by blissful inch until I've never felt so full.

Max sets a steady, almost gentle pace. Gliding out and thrusting back into me with strokes that leave me quivering. Drawing out the pleasure, and fuck, what pleasure it is. It's like he knows exactly what to do to leave me moaning, when to fuck me harder, and when to leave me strung out on the edge.

"Please," I'm gasping. "Oh God, don't stop."

"Never." His voice is a low growl in my ear. Max slams into me again, harder this time. "Fuck, Hallie, you feel so good. I've never been with anyone who makes me feel like you do."

He thrusts deeper, his cock hitting that special spot inside, and my answer is lost in a moan. I'm almost beyond words now. "Me too." I manage to hold on tight. "Oh, God. Right there. Don't stop."

And he doesn't. I'm so close, so fucking close, and then Max pauses, and grasps my chin, turning my face up to meet his heavy-lidded gaze, and fuck, just seeing the pure, animal desire in his eyes is too much for me. I come undone just like that, losing my breath in the surge of pleasure that crashes over me, again and again. Max groans, and with a shudder, he follows me over the edge.

Damn. That was . . .

Incredible. Epic.

Real.

Max collapses beside me, and then wordlessly tugs me into his arms to spoon. I snuggle back against him, perfectly worn out. My eyes are starting to glaze over as my gaze drifts around the room. It's practically as fancy as our guest suite. Cushy couches, framed pictures all over the walls. Trust Franklin Carlisle to turn even his beach cabana into an art gallery . . .

Somewhere in my half-asleep brain, a memory sparks.

Carlisle publications have always been a window to the world. In fact, this very building used to be the tallest in the city, before the Empire State Building was constructed.

My pulse stutters. I sit up with a jolt.

"What?" Max asks, raising his head.

"I think I know where the prize is." My heart beats faster. "The Carlisle Publishing building in New York!"

I quickly explain about my conversation with Ernest, what seems like a hundred years ago . . . but was only last week. "There's a gallery there, that's what he could mean. The photographs are the windows to the world. "

Max's eyes widen. "That could be it. No wonder he's been laughing at us for hanging around here."

My brain is already two steps ahead. "Do you think we can get out of here to investigate without anyone noticing?"

Max grins. "Oh, I know how to go into full-on stealth mode. We'll be in New York before they even realize we're gone."

20

HALLIE

THE TAXI CROSSES the bridge into downtown Manhattan just as the dawn glow is lighting the streets. Even to my bleary eyes, it's a gorgeous sight. I stifle a yawn, taking in the pinkish tinge reflecting off the skyscrapers, the streets that are about as quiet as Manhattan ever gets. My head feels muggy, I didn't manage to sleep more than three hours of sleep on the plane, but my heart is thumping with anticipation.

We're close. This is the final treasure location, it has to be.

My stomach grumbles, and Max looks over with a smile. "Hungry?"

"First the treasure, then breakfast," I say firmly.

"You always did have your priorities straight." He glances out the window. "I love the city this early in the morning. Like the calm before the storm. We should go to Cairo sometime," he adds. "There's a spot near one of the markets, best coffee I've ever had in my life and great food too. The way the light hits the buildings around there as the sun is just rising . . ." He smiles at me. "You'll love it."

"Oh," I say, as casually as I can manage, pretending my heart isn't flipping over at the mention of future plans. Our future. "That sounds amazing."

"Have you ever been?"

I shake my head. "I've tagged along to Europe. And to Tokyo once. But that was all business—assisting at conferences and that sort of thing. I didn't get to do a whole lot of sightseeing."

"Then we've got a lot of catching up to do." Max squeezes my hand. "I'm looking forward to it."

I can't help beaming back at him. My throat suddenly feels tight with emotion, but it's a good kind of emotion. I haven't wanted to ask if our not-so-fake relationship will see out the week, but it seems like Max is thinking the exact same thing as me.

That this, whatever crazy way it started, is something real now. Something special.

The cab pulls up outside the building, and he pays the driver before we climb out.

"Ready?" Max looks as tense and excited as I feel. After all, there's nothing between him and a billion-dollar inheritance now. We took extra care to sneak out of the estate without anyone noticing. We left on foot, hailing a cab a mile down the road to take us to the airport, grabbing the first red-eye flight that would take us out here. 007's got nothing on us.

"Ready." We push past the massive doors and stop in the majestic foyer. That moment when I stood here before my interview feels like it was a year ago, not just a week.

The gallery is closed, a little sign hanging in the frosted glass window.

"What exactly did the last clue say again?" I ask.

He brings it up on his phone. *"From inside and above, it's a window to the world. Arrive to see it first, and you'll find your prize unfurled."*

"Inside *and* above," I repeat. "So it could be the gallery or the roof. There's an observation deck up there . . ."

"77 floors," Max says. "That really narrows it down. Well, why don't we start at the top and work our way from there."

We get in the elevator, my pulse thumping faster. I can almost taste it: our victory—well, Max's victory, but it feels like mine too—waiting for us up there.

"Nervous?" I ask Max.

He kisses me. "Not anymore. I'm ready for this," he says, and I know he doesn't just mean winning. He's ready to take control of the company, and take it in the right direction, and I know he'll do an amazing job.

The elevator stops at the top floor, and the door opens.

"So, you finally made it."

We stop dead. The observation deck is full. Artie, Cordelia, Parker and Brad, plus a couple of their SWAT team looking guys, and a few dudes in suits for good measure. There's barely enough room for us to get out of the elevator.

Artie steps forward with a sneer. "Haven't I always told you, Max: never fly commercial. It takes twice as long, and you can miss out on all the breaks."

He holds up another linen envelope—but this one is twice as big as the clues, with a fancy wax seal. A seal that's clearly been broken. "In this case, the jet saved us a fortune. And lost you one. Whoops."

My heart sinks. Beside me, Max is rigid. "How the hell did you get here in time?" he demands. "You guys were stuck back at the estate! You had no idea where to look!"

Artie chortles. "All thanks to your lovely fiancée. Thanks for the intel, Hallie." He winks. "We never would have beaten him without you."

Wait, what?

Before I can sputter a response, Artie has snapped his fingers to summon his crew. "Enough chit-chat. We've got celebrating to do—and a business to sell."

They brush past us to the elevator. "But, you're lying!" I protest. "I never—"

Ding!

The doors close behind them. Max and I are left alone.

"You need to tell me what the hell is going on."

Max's voice is like steel. I turn. He's staring at me like I'm a stranger.

"I don't know!" I protest. "I swear I didn't tell them. He *tried* to bribe me into helping him, days ago, but I told him to stick his offer up his ass. Max, you have to believe me!"

"He knew to come here," Max says slowly. "Not just the city, but this building. Right after we figured it out. No one even knew we'd left. And why would he thank you if you had nothing to do with it?"

I throw my hands in the air. "I don't know! Because he's an asshole. I have no idea how he figured it out, but I swear it had nothing to do with me. Why would I sabotage you when we were so close?"

"Maybe he offered you more money than I did," Max says darkly. "What's your price then? A hundred grand? A million? You were only doing this for the money anyway. So why not go with the highest bidder?"

I feel like I've just been hit in the gut. "That's not the kind of person I am. I wouldn't do that to anyone." A swell of emotion fills my throat. "I wouldn't do that to *you*."

But Max is still looking at me like the past week means nothing. He shakes his head. "I thought that was true. I thought— For fuck's sake, Hallie, I trusted you with everything. So you can stop lying. Just admit it. What was your price?"

I don't know what to say to make him believe me. I don't know if *I'd* believe me if our positions were reversed. Ten minutes ago, everything felt perfect. How can it all have come crashing down so fast?

My eyes well up. I swipe at them, fighting to keep my voice steady. "I'm not lying. I didn't sell you out. If you trusted me before, then keep trusting me. We can look into it, try to figure out how he—"

"No," Max snaps. "I don't ever want to see you again. Enjoy your dirty money."

He turns on his heel and stalks away. "Max, please, listen to me!" I desperately follow and grab him by the arm. He jerks around. His eyes are so hard with anger they freeze me in place.

"Why did you even take this job?"

"What?"

"You heard me. I asked you before, back when all of this was just beginning, and you said you'd tell me later. Well, now is later. So?"

I falter. "I . . . I . . ."

Max stares at me, waiting.

"I thought, maybe, I could show my photographs to someone," I confess, my cheeks flushing red. "I applied for a job at one of your magazines, and didn't get it. I just wanted a chance," I add miserably. "To be judged on my talent."

"And you do have ample *talents*, don't you?"

My head snaps up. "That isn't fair."

"Why not? You said it yourself, you were using me from the start. But why settle for a couple of photography assignments when you could take a slice of the whole company?"

"No." I gulp, my tears coming now. "It's not like that!"

"I know exactly how it is." Max's angry expression drops, just for a moment, and I see the betrayal in his eyes.

Somehow, that's worse.

"I trusted you, Hallie." His face twists with emotion. "I thought you were different from these vultures. Someone real. But I guess I was wrong."

He gets on the elevator before I can say another word. The doors slide shut, and then he's gone.

I sink down onto one of the deck's benches and drop my face into my hands. The tears stream out with a sob I can't control. It's over. I've lost it all. The guy, the company that should have been his, the dream he was building for his future . . .

But I still don't understand how any of it happened.

At last, my sobs subside, but I don't even know what to do next. My stuff is still in Palm Beach, but I can't face going back there. And how? This was all Max's mission: I was just along for the ride.

Don't let yourself get swept up in the moment, Olivia told me. *It's purely business.* I wish I'd listened to her. Maybe then I wouldn't feel like I've lost the best man I've ever known.

Hello, heartbreak. Population: me.

21

HALLIE

"WHY ARE you sitting on the couch upside down?"

Jules's footsteps stop by my nose. She peers down at me. It's kind of hard to look her in the eyes with my head tipped back toward the floor. "I don't know. I thought maybe a little more blood to the brain could get me out of my funk. That's a thing, right?"

"I'm not sure it's a typical cure for broken hearts, no," Jules says, sounding amused. She sits down beside me. "Is it working?"

"No. Mostly it's just making me feel dizzy." I turn the right way up and sigh. It's been two weeks since Max left me on that rooftop, and my heart still hurts like it was five minutes ago. "This is ridiculous," I wail. "I hardly knew him. Aren't there rules about that?"

"I think it's a month of grieving for every year you dated," Jules says, looking amused.

"So I should have been over him in, like, two hours." I slump lower.

"So you haven't heard anything at all from him?"

"No," I say mournfully. "He thinks I screwed him over. Which I didn't. I mean, I screwed him, but—the good way."

Jules muffles a snicker. "Yeah, I had gathered that part."

I kick the cushion, which probably isn't fair, since *it's* never done anything to me. "What's wrong with me? I knew from the start he was too charming for my own good. No strings, Mr. Love 'Em and Leave 'Em."

Except that wasn't the real Max. No, the man behind that devastating smile was kind, and funny, and sweet . . .

I turn and scream into a pillow.

Jules pats my head sympathetically. "I'm sorry, babe. I never thought you'd lose your head like this. Or your heart."

"It just . . . happened." I sniffle. "It seemed like he was feeling the same way. Like there was something real there." My heart still aches, just remembering the betrayal on Max's face right before he walked away from me.

"Maybe it was real," Jules says gently. "He wouldn't have been that angry with you if he didn't care."

I don't know what to believe. "Either way, it's over. He still thinks I sold him out."

"Well, the truth is on your side," Jules says. "Maybe it's weird for me to say this as a lawyer, but sometimes that does matter, no matter how much other people try to bend it. The truth will come out, and then he'll realize what a mistake he made not trusting you."

"That's the part that really hurts," I admit. "I mean, I know it looked bad, with what Artie said. But part of me feels betrayed too. He should have believed me."

"So, don't let this guy keep you down," Jules says brightly. "Get out of the apartment. Take a walk. And maybe take a shower first."

"Is that a hint?" I ask wryly.

She grins. "Hate to break it to you, babe, but those sweatpants are crying out for the laundry."

I look down and grimace. "Maybe you're right."

There's a knock on the apartment door. Jules goes to answer it. A guy in a courier uniform is standing on the other side. "Delivery for Hallie Gage," he says, brandishing a thick envelope. "I need your signature."

I sign his clipboard and look over the envelope. There's no sender address on it.

"Well, open it already," Jules urges.

I tear open the seal and pull out the papers inside. There's a statement of contract fulfillment—and a check for fifty thousand dollars, signed by—

"Max Carlisle."

I gulp.

"You still got paid!" Jules crows. "At least something good came out of all that craziness."

"But . . ." I shake my head. "I can't take this. I can't believe he even paid me after what happened."

Jules shrugged. "He probably didn't have a choice. If his contract with The Agency was half as good as yours, it was watertight. You spent a week with him as his fake girlfriend. Job fulfilled."

Maybe so, but the check still doesn't feel right, clutched there in my hand. I grab my purse and shove it in. "I think I'll take that walk."

I SHOWER AND change into something vaguely human, and head uptown to the Agency. Approaching the brownstone building, my stomach ties in knots. If I hadn't run into Olivia—if I hadn't taken her up on her offer—I never would have gotten involved in Max's whole crazy life. He would be a hot, steamy memory from the wedding, and nothing more.

But I was the one who said yes, I remind myself. And kept saying it, despite all the lines I was burring.

And even after everything, I can't regret him. Not one moment.

I hit the buzzer. Alice's chirpy voice carries through the intercom. "The Agency. Who's calling?"

"It's Hallie," I say. "I need to talk to Olivia. Is she there?"

"Come on up, Hallie," Alice says without hesitation. Huh. I wonder if Olivia was expecting me to come calling. I haven't talked to her since everything fell apart with Max. I figured he'd fill her in on the story however he wanted to. I don't really enjoy the thought of hashing it out all over again, but I head up the stairs all the same. Like before, Alice opens the door before I've reached the top. She gives me a bright smile. "Hi, how are you doing? Did you change your hair? I like it."

"Um, thanks." I step into the office, immediately surrounded by understated luxury. Thor even comes over to batter my calf with one of his affectionate head-butts.

Olivia's office door opens. "Hallie." She beckons me over, and I brace myself. Why does it feel like I'm visiting the headmaster's office? Maybe something about how effortlessly elegant Olivia looks, ushering me to a chair and carefully pouring us tea.

"So," Olivia says. "I hear things with Max Carlisle didn't end too well?"

"Understatement of the year." I cringe. "I'm sorry. I know you warned me, but I didn't follow your rules. I didn't even follow mine," I say sadly. "But I swear, I don't know what he told you, but it was a misunderstanding. I never went behind his back about anything."

"I never said you did," Olivia says calmly.

"But what am I supposed to do with this?"

I pull out the check, and put it on the polished coffee table between us.

"Deposit it?" Olivia arches an eyebrow. "I assume he's good for the funds."

"You know what I mean. I let the lines get blurred! I was trying to stay totally professional," I add. "But . . . he grew on me. Like fungus. I really liked him," I add miserably. "And . . . one thing led to another. A few times."

Olivia eyes me carefully. "Casual hook-ups have been known to happen in this business, but it doesn't sound like this was so casual."

Suddenly I'm wondering exactly what Max told her. But that's not a healthy path for me to go down. "No," I admit. "I fell for him. That sounds pathetic, doesn't it? You told me to remember it wasn't real and I went head over heels anyway."

"I'm sorry," Olivia says, "I threw you in the deep end with this assignment. Perhaps I should have found someone else, someone more experienced."

"With resisting playboys, or jet-setting treasure hunts?"

Her lips quirk in a smile. "Perhaps both."

"Either way, I can't accept this." I nudge the check closer to her. Olivia's brow knits.

"But it's yours," she says. "You earned that money. Why on earth shouldn't you take it?"

"Well . . ." It seems so obvious to me, but now that I have to put it into words, I'm fumbling. "It just feels wrong. The time I was with him didn't feel like work. I wanted to be there. And then the way things ended . . ."

Olivia takes the check, puts it back in my hand, and closes her fingers over mine. "Hallie," she says, looking me straight in the eyes, "you deserve this. I know you've had an upset here—"

Understatement of the year.

"—but the best thing you can do now is move on," she finishes. "Go ahead, build the photography career you were dreaming about. That was the point of all of this, after all."

A very compelling argument. I waver, but I don't know how to argue with the full force of her firm gaze on me. "I'll think about it," I finally agree.

Olivia smiles. "Now, I have an appointment coming . . ."

"Of course." I bob up. "And thanks, for everything. I know I made a mess of it, but I appreciate you trying to help."

"My pleasure. And chin up," Olivia adds. "Love happens to the best of us."

Love?

I make it down the stairs and out the front door before the word catches up with me. My legs balk. I sit down on the front steps, clutching my purse. I feel stranded, and I don't know what to do.

Is this really how I want to start my photography studio? I know it's different, but somehow using Max's money feels just as bad as if I *had* scammed him out of his inheritance.

I can't make up my mind either way. Finally, after a few minutes, the door whispers open behind me.

"Enjoying the view?" Alice asks.

"Sorry, am I blocking the entry? I'm just trying to make a decision that could change the whole course of my life," I sigh. "It's a lot of pressure. There really should be a guidebook or something."

She sits beside me. "You know, whenever I'm in a bind, I always think of what my dad used to say. 'You already know the answer.' "

"I really don't."

Alice laughs. "I know, that's what I would always reply. But, he was right. Annoyingly so."

I pause. Maybe she has a point. I mean, I already know I can live with being poor and scraping my way up the ladder. I've done that already. I *don't* think I can live with leaping to the top of that ladder knowing I only got there with a boost from Max Carlisle, with him hating me the whole while.

"Thank you," I say, standing up. I hand her the check. "Tell Olivia I appreciated her advice, but I really can't accept this. I'd like her to send it back to Max."

"Are you sure?" Alice looks stunned.

"Completely." Just like that, a weight is lifted off me. I take in a deep breath, feeling almost okay for the first time in two weeks.

I'm halfway to the subway when my phone rings. I fish it out of my purse. "Hello?"

"This is Lydia Burns from Carlisle Publishing," the crisp voice on the other end says. "Are you available to come in for a meeting today, Miss Gage?"

22

HALLIE

I STAND on the sidewalk outside the Carlisle Building, my stomach tied up in knots. It's got to be Max, hasn't it? The secretary on the phone was vague about the meeting, so maybe Jules is right. He's figured out that I had nothing to do with Artie's backstabbing, and he invited me here to apologize and make it all OK.

In your dreams.

I head inside and security directs me up to the same floor where I had my interview—and there's Ms. Editor with her frizzy curls. I give her a polite smile and look around for Max. But she plants herself in front of me and extends her hand.

"Hallie, I'm glad you could make it in on such short notice."

Oh. "*You* called the meeting?" I ask, trying to hide my disappointment.

She blinks. "Well, yes. Did my secretary not make that clear?" She sighs. "I'm sorry, I'm training in someone new this week. Would you come into my office?"

I follow her, curious now.

"I know we couldn't find a place for you in Art," the editor says.

"But it turns out we have a position as a photography assistant that's just opened up." She rolls her eyes. "So much turnover these days. No one knows how to commit to a job.."

I straighten up. "So . . . is this another interview? I'm sorry, I didn't bring my portfolio. If you want, I—"

Ms. Editor waves me off. "It's fine. The position's yours if you still want it. I know I liked what I saw."

She *did*? Could have fooled me. I'd hate to see how she looks through a portfolio she doesn't like.

Hold on, did she just say—

"I have the job?" I repeat, my eyes widening.

"Yes," the editor says, sounding amused. "I take it you are interested."

"Yes. Yes, absolutely." A photo assistant position here at Carlisle Publishing—it doesn't even matter what magazine or paper it's for, it's a big leap up that ladder. Holy shit. It's really happening.

With awfully coincidental timing. I pause, my pulse skipping. "This might sound like a strange question, but did Max have anything to do with this?"

Ms. Editor raises one carefully plucked eyebrow. "Max? I'm not sure who you're thinking about, but this offer is straight from me."

Oh. That last bit of hope snuffs out. But still. This is the job I wanted. Like the universe telling me I made the right decision handing back that check.

"Never mind," I say quickly. "I'm so happy a spot opened up. When do I start?"

The editor smiles. "Next Monday, if you can."

"I'll be here!"

I leave with all the details, still in a daze. But even though I'm grateful for the chance, I still have this ache of pain lingering in my chest. I want to be happy, it's just hard to be overjoyed after the romantic roller coaster I've just been on. And the weirdest part is that all I want to do right now is call Max and tell him about the job. I can imagine how he'd have cheered at my victory, and insisted that of course they would be wowed by my talent . . .

I shake it off, but my heart is still heavy.

Back in the lobby, I can't quite bear to leave yet. Instead I wander into the gallery. I drift from display to display, soaking the images in. It's ridiculous, I realize. That treasure hunt Franklin Carlisle sent his family on was all about the history and legacy of his company. But now scheming Artie and the rest of them will tear all that history down.

I hope it was worth it.

This time I hear the curator's soft shuffling before he completely sneaks up on me. Ernest Hammersmith is looking as cheerfully Santa Claus-y as ever.

"The photographer," he beams. "You came back. Looking for inspiration?"

"Celebrating," I reply. "I just got hired on as a photo assistant."

His eyes light up. "Well, then. Congratulations!" Then his enthusiasm dims. "I hope it survives the shakeup, when the company changes hands."

He already knows? My stomach clenches. "I know Franklin Carlisle is passing it on. Is the sale already a sure thing?"

"It might as well be. That Arthur Junior is a piece of work," he adds ruefully. "He's been pushing to unload the whole place for years."

Damn. Even though I knew it was coming, it still hurts. "I'm really sorry about that," I say. "I can tell the company means a lot to you."

"To be sure. I'm one of the board members, you know," he adds. "Won some shares off Franklin in a hand of cards, forty years ago now."

"No, really?"

But Ernest doesn't look so happy. "Carlisle Publishing has been a profitable and respected business for nearly a century. None of us wants to see it stripped for parts. But the younger generation, they've got no interest in learning the ropes and putting in the hard work to keep up that tradition. They just want to make a quick buck."

I pause, trying to remember what I heard Artie say, that night at the party. He had some of the board members on his side, ready for when he got his hands on Franklin's shares.

Does this mean he couldn't sell without them?

"How is the ownership of the company split?" I demand, my excitement rising. "Franklin's portion isn't enough to make that call on its own, is it? If you all stood up and fought to keep things the way they are—"

Ernest sighs. "In theory. But as you can see, we're all getting on. Franklin was the real force behind things. Without him, there's no real leadership."

"Well, here's hoping there's still a company—and a job for me—come Monday," I say, rueful.

Ernest smiles. "I hope to see you soon."

I exit, my happiness dimmed even more. I hate to imagine what Artie and co. will do to the Carlisle legacy, so how must Max be feeling, watching everything fall apart?

Nope, I'm not supposed to be thinking about him. The whole point of getting out of the house was to clear my head. And now that I've returned the money, I don't have any ties to him.

Clean break. Fresh start.

So how can I explain ambling up to Central Park? And if I happen to stroll toward the Boathouse where my camera—and the rest of me—took that unfortunate tumble the other week, that's just a coincidence too. I'm absolutely not scanning the lawns trying to pick out the exact spot where the refreshment tent was set up. The spot where I first locked eyes with Max Carlisle.

I sit down and gaze out across the lake. I replay our first meeting over again—his cocky grin, our banter, dear Lord, that amazing kiss . . .

I never would have thought I'd fall for the guy I met over those cupcakes. Every red flag was waving that I knew his type. But I was wrong. There's so much more to him than the cocky charmer he seemed at first glance.

Is he even thinking of me at all? Or has he moved on to the next foreign assignment, the next no-strings girl, like I never existed at all?

It's a good thing I'm not the gambling kind, because the cruel truth is, I would bet everything that he hasn't skipped a beat.

23

MAX

I LINE up a serve and slam the ball at the playing wall. It careens off the corner and ricochets so hard, I have to leap out of the way.

My buddy Cal snorts. "My point. Again."

I scowl.

Usually, a game of racquetball with a buddy is all I need to clear my mind and unwind.

Usually, I'm not dealing with betrayal, backstabbing, and the end of the Carlisle family legacy as we know it.

Cal pauses to take a drink of water. "Not that I'm not enjoying the spectacle, but you're sucking more than usual today."

"Real supportive," I growl.

"Oh, I'm sorry." Cal smirks. "Did you want to sit and talk about your feelings?"

I scowl harder. Cal and I go way back, he's CEO of the McAdams auto empire, and usually, he understands the shit I'm going through with my family. But he can't understand this.

"Let's just play."

"Your funeral." Cal tosses me the ball. "It almost makes me wish I was a betting man."

I snort. "Since when did you quit the blackjack table?" Cal is usually the first on the casino floor, off following the racing circuit in Monte Carlo, Montreal, and more.

"Since I'm a new man," Cal replies easily. "Shaping up my reputation."

"And how's that working out?"

"About as well as your racquetball game."

I grip my handle and serve again. This time, I manage a couple of shots before I slam the damn thing out of bounds.

"I'm fine!" I exclaim, before Cal can needle me again.

"Clearly," he replies. "But since this face is too pretty to break, how about we take this to the bar?"

Tempting. But I've spent the past two weeks trying to drink away this hole in my heart, and it hasn't worked yet.

"Another time," I say reluctantly. "I have a meeting with my lawyers at three."

Cal arches an eyebrow. "Any luck getting that treasure hunt thrown out?"

"Not so far," I sigh. "But maybe they've found some loophole."

"You know, I always knew your grandfather was eccentric, but this?" Cal and I head for the locker room. "It's like he's burning down everything he's built just to prove a point."

"A bone-headed, idiotic point." I shake my head. "He spent his life building and protecting the company, and he's just handing it off to Artie because he got to the final clue two minutes before me."

Thanks to Hallie's treacherous twist, that is.

"Well, if you need a job, just let me know," Cal says. "I'm sure I can find something for you. How do you like Monaco in the spring?"

"Thanks, but I'm fine. It's the rest of the employees I'm worried about."

Cal winces. "Yeah, that can't be fun. The business press is already buzzing about Carlisle sales and lay-offs."

"Vultures."

"But who can blame them for the wild speculation?" Cal points out. "After all, this is the biggest story in the industry right now."

"And they don't even know the half of it."

I think of Hallie again, and the lead weight returns to my gut. I still can't believe she sold me out like that.

And I still don't understand why.

I didn't see it coming, that's for sure. There I was, making future plans. Actually imagining my life with her in it. The travel, the adventure. The hot, smoking sex. And a connection, too, something realer than I'd ever felt before. It was like she was the first person to know me, really know me.

It just turned out I didn't know her at all.

I SHOWER AND CHANGE, and then head over to my lawyer's office. They've been at war with the rest of my cousins' legal teams since this whole treasure hunt finished. I know I should just give it up and move on; hell, it's a philosophy I've spent most of my life follow-ing. No strings, no complications, just a damn good time. Easy.

But it turns out leaving was only easy because I never cared about anything I lost.

Great timing, Max. I picked the perfect moment to understand my family legacy—the responsibility it took to lead the company and keep the tradition of excellence alive. And I chose an even better moment to want it.

Right when Hallie plucked it out of my grasp for good.

Her face slips into my thoughts again, and damn, it hurts. Her innocent act was so good, I might have bought it if Artie hadn't given the game away.

Did she really believe that snake would let her get off scot-free? That I'd never find out? Or was the plan just to make a quick escape and leave me hanging, never knowing why?

I was so stupid, letting her get under my skin. From the start, it was a simple arrangement. Fake the emotions, take the money. Hell,

I'm the one who proposed it that way! I didn't realize the spell she'd cast over me, drawing me in with her smart mouth, and determined spirit, that tempting gleam in her eyes.

And as for her body . . .

I shake my head. Yeah, nothing good can come of reliving *those* nights together. At least, not without another cold shower. And right now, I need my head in the game if there's any last hope of stopping Artie's takeover—and the end of Carlisle Publishing.

"Max," Anthony greets me when I get off the elevator. He's the senior partner who handles most of my affairs. "How's my favorite publishing dynasty scion?"

"Soon to be former," I point out. "Unless you've found some miracle Hail Mary play?"

"Why don't we take a seat?" he says.

That would be a no, then.

I follow him to his office. "Unfortunately, there's no law against deciding ownership by treasure hunt," he says. "Your grandfather's shares are his to do with as he wishes. In fact, by doing this while he was still alive, he left even fewer avenues to contest. If he were dead, we could argue incapacity, or undue influence by your cousins. But, alive, he's clearly making the decision for himself."

"As to the matter of how fairly the victory was obtained . . ." Anthony goes on. "I've investigated that side of the situation thoroughly. I don't think we can make a case based on the actions of an independent party acting of her own accord."

That being the independent party of Hallie. I let out my breath. "So, it's gone, then. They really won."

Anthony gives me a sympathetic smile. "That's about the size of it. I could come up with some trumped up accusations to maybe delay the passing of the torch for months, maybe even a few years. But it's my responsibility to tell you up front you've got no hope in hell of them doing anything more than delaying."

"Shit." I sink back. "So, they'll sell it off, and the new owners will strip the company for parts."

"If they get the requisite votes from the board, yes."

That's it then. Game over. Only, it isn't a game anymore.

"Thanks all the same," I say, getting to my feet.

"One more thing." Anthony retrieves an envelope. "This came for you."

I tear it open. When I see what's inside, I freeze.

It's Hallie's contract. And the check.

I take it out, staring at it. Fifty thousand dollars. And she sent it back? "This came from *her*?" I demand.

"It came by way of The Agency. Apparently, she refused payment. That should help defray a few of your costs," Anthony says brightly. "And on that note, perhaps we can set up a time to discuss your investments—"

"Later," I say shortly. "I'll see you soon."

I walk out, still holding the check tightly. Why the hell would she reject the payment? She was only in this for the money the whole time.

Maybe Artie's payoff was so big, she didn't need my trifling contribution. Figured she'd rub it in my face—or show me charity, since clearly I'm missing out on the big fortune.

But that doesn't make sense. Hallie might have sold me out, but she was never vindictive about it. If she'd wanted to lord it over me, she could have done so right there on the observation deck instead of pretending she had no clue what was going on.

That's not the kind of person I am. I wouldn't do that to anyone. I wouldn't do that to you.

Guilt gnaws at me again. Either she's an Oscar-worthy actress, or . . .

Or, there's something else going on.

I look at the rejected check again. Something just isn't right about this. And it's going to eat away at me until I know the truth.

I hail a cab and climb in. "Take me to the Carlisle building."

I HAVEN'T BEEN BACK since the day of the hunt, but I brace myself and head for the top floors. Executive level. I figure Artie won't have wasted any time upgrading his office to Franklin's palatial corner suite, and sure enough, he's just seeing out a bunch of older men and women I recognize from the board. "I'm sure we'll come to an agreement that everyone is happy with," he's saying.

"I need some more time to think about this," one of the board members says, sounding uncertain.

Artie smiles briskly. "It really will work in all of our favor, if you just consider—"

His sees me, and his lips curl into his habitual smirk. "Max. What a surprise."

"I need to talk to you." I manage to sound civil.

"Anything for a dear cousin," Artie says with a saccharine tone. He waves off the board members and motions me into the office.

"Like what I've done with the place?" Artie crows.

It looks like an English hunting lodge threw up in here. Fake deer trophies on the wall, tartan and wood everywhere, and there's even one of those goddamned German shepherd statues Cordelia loves sitting in the corner.

I shouldn't be surprised. All the money in the world still can't buy this jackass taste.

"Meeting with the board?" I ask instead. "Don't tell me you haven't drummed up enough votes for a sale yet. You've been saying for years they'll jump if they have the chance."

Artie scowls. "Already taken care of," he says. "I have them in the palm of my hand. We meet to vote next week, and then this company will be someone else's problem. And we'll all be a hell of a lot richer. Well, except you, of course." He smirks.

"If you say so."

Artie goes to shuffle papers on his desk, clearly trying to look important. "What do you want, Max? Here to grovel and beg for a piece of the action?"

"Actually, I was just wondering about something," I say, running my finger idly along the edge of the window frame. The less this seems to matter to me, the more likely Artie will tell me the truth. "What did it take to buy off Hallie, anyway?"

"Oh, is *that* what's on your mind?" Artie's voice turns into a sneer. "Thought you knew her so well, didn't you?"

I raise my eyes. "Yeah," I say calmly. "I did. You really got one over on me there."

"It wasn't hard at all, I can tell you that," Artie says, leaning back against the desk looking smug. "You two were never equipped to play in the big leagues with the rest of us."

"Guess not," I agree, even though I want to smack that smile off his face. "So what did you do to turn her around to your side?"

Artie chuckles. "What the hell, it can't hurt to tell you now. The bitch was too hung up on you to respond to reason anyway. But we didn't need her to play along, not once I had a bug planted on her phone."

"What?" I stare at him in disbelief.

"My guy hooked me up, we planted it once you beat us back to Palm Beach. Easy. It didn't just get her calls, but anything you guys said in the room. The minute she cracked that last clue, we were on the jet for New York." Artie grins. "Never saw *that* coming, did you, Mr. Adventure?"

His words hit me like a punch to the gut. They didn't turn Hallie? They tried and she *refused*?

My hands clench again. A hot flush is rising through me that's both anger and shame. Anger at Artie. Shame that I didn't believe Hallie when she tried to tell me she was innocent.

"No," I grit out. "I didn't see it coming. I didn't think even you would stoop quite that low."

The anger floods through me, and I lunge at him. In a second, I've got him pinned to the wall by his lapels. "You see that deer head?" I ground out, shaking him furiously. "I'm going to mount your sorry ass right beside it!"

"Help!" Artie shrieks. "Security!"

Two guys come rushing in and drag me off him. My heart is pounding.

"I'll have you arrested for this!" Artie is flushed and quaking. "Get out of my building!"

"With pleasure."

I stalk out, furious, but as the elevator heads back down to street-level, the anger shifts. I'm not mad at Artie for lying and cheating. No, I'm mad at myself for believing him.

God, how much have I fucked up? Hallie was on my side the whole time. And I threw her loyalty back in her face. I didn't even give her a real chance to talk it through with me. I told her I never wanted to see her again. She was fucking *crying* and I left her there.

Is there anything I can do to make this right?

24

HALLIE

"OKAY, now why don't we get you leaning against the window frame, looking right at the camera. Yes, perfect."

Melissa Hudson, the photographer I've been assigned to assist, snaps several photos of the actress. One of Carlisle Publishing's entertainment magazines is doing a story on Laura London. She drapes herself elegantly against the window, doing an excellent impression of the lady victim of consumption she got an Oscar nomination for portraying. I'm not sure if it's on purpose, but the romantically frail look is working for her.

Melissa looks equally cool in a totally different way. With her spiky hair and leather jacket, she could have walked out of a punk concert. She takes her shots with a practiced efficiency—always focused, always poised with complete confidence.

I so want to be her when I grow up.

When Melissa pauses to skim through the photos on her view screen, I hop up on a chair to adjust the position of one of the lights. "Oh, that's perfect, Hallie," she says when she glances up. "Good call."

I grin as I hop down. "I was thinking, maybe if she sat on the ledge with her face right by the glass—you'd get that extra glow from outside."

Melissa nods with a thoughtful expression. "Nice. I'm going to get a few more like this and then we'll try that. Since it was your idea, do you want to take some of the shots? You might as well get that practice."

"Oh, wow, thank you!" I say, practically beaming now. I've only been working with Melissa for a few days, and I already feel like I've learned twice as much as I did assisting guys like Frederico for six months. She knows her stuff and she's great at what she does—and she's not at all bothered by lending a hand to someone on the way up. I really couldn't have asked for my dream job to be any more dreamy.

However long it might last. The rest of the staff has been buzzing about the fate of Carlisle Publishing all week, and it knots my stomach every time I think of it. Not just because of my own job, but because of what Max must be feeling.

Does he still blame me? Is he out there somewhere, cursing my name? Or, worse, is he on a beach with some bikini model, forgetting that I even exist?

"Let's get some shots on the chair now," Melissa says, bringing me back to my assignment. "Wardrobe, can you fluff the dress?"

The actress moves into position, and a cluster of stylists help rearrange her outfit. No wonder I can never make my clothes look as good as in the magazines—they have a whole team pinning and tucking to make sure—

My heart stops. A figure's just appeared in the doorway.

It can't be . . .

But it is. Max steps into the room, as casual and confident as ever. I haven't seen him in three weeks, and somehow I forgot how fucking hot he is.

What is he doing here?

I gulp for air. One thing I'm sure of: Whatever he's got to say, I don't think I want to have that conversation in front of my new boss. I hurry over to meet him before he can start yelling at me again.

"Max." I stop short in front of him, and that ache in my chest goes up to 11. I'm not sure I even want to give him a hello. Shit, how's my hair? I haven't looked in a mirror in hours and I've been scrambling all over arranging the sets. I rake my fingers back through it.

It shouldn't matter. But it does. But I definitely don't want him realizing it does.

"Hallie," he says. His voice is still just as panty-melting too, that low slightly rough baritone. He runs a hand over his own hair, looking as if maybe I'm not the only one feeling awkward here. My nerves settle just a little.

"Do you have a minute?" he asks, holding my gaze with the blue-gray eyes that captivated me from the first time I met him. "I was hoping we could talk."

A very large part of me screams *Yes!* The rest of me knows better. *He* walked out on *me*—after believing I was a backstabbing duplicitous bitch. I'm not the one who needs to grovel here. And I'm sure as hell not risking my dream job to hear what might just be more accusations.

"We've got another hour to go here," I say, impressed by how steady I keep my voice. "But I might have time after."

"Whatever works for you," he says. "I'll be right outside."

Well, that wasn't so hard. I jog back over to where Melissa is at work and try to refocus on the job. But it's hard, knowing that Max is just a few feet away. But I force myself to concentrate, even when we run over schedule. I gulp, wondering if he'll wait that long, but after handshakes and goodbyes, I come out of the room to find Max still waiting. He gets up from the bench in the hall and hesitates, like he's not sure he's welcome even now.

I'm not sure he is either. I cross my arms over my chest, trying to look fierce. I feel like I need a shield. I thought I'd gotten over the battering my heart took, but suddenly it feels tender all over again.

"It looks like there's a little courtyard out back where we could talk," Max suggests.

I nod and follow him out. The yard is small but picturesque, with a wrought-iron fence twined with flowering vines. Max tucks his hands in his pockets as if he's not sure what to do with them. He looks at the lawn and then at me.

"I don't know where to start except to say I'm sorry," he says. "I'm sorry I didn't believe you. I'm sorry I listened to Artie instead of you. I should have known you wouldn't do that to me, whatever the price . . . I talked to him," he adds ruefully. "He had a bug on your phone. That's how they knew where we'd gone."

The breath I've been holding rushes out of me. Max knows I didn't do anything wrong. He knows I didn't lie!

But something in me holds back from celebrating. Apparently, it took Artie's confession for Max to change his mind. Not anything to do with me. What I said, everything we did together—none of that counted for anything.

"You shouldn't have needed Artie's explanation," I say, fighting to keep my voice even. "Maybe we hadn't been together that long, but I thought you knew me better than that. But instead, you took his word over mine."

Max hangs his head. "I know," he says. "I don't know what to tell you. I was so caught up in the treasure hunt, I wasn't thinking straight. I fucked up. You don't need to convince me of that. You have no idea how sorry I am."

He raises his head to meet my gaze again. The regret in his eyes hits me straight in the heart. "Losing you was almost as bad as losing the company." Max confesses. "No, actually it was worse. I can build another company if I want to. But I know I'll never find another you."

Oh shit. I curl my fingers into my palms, and try to stay strong. He's saying this now, but it's easy to say things. How am I ever going to know he means them?

I clear my throat. "What's happening with Carlisle Publishing?" I ask. "Am I going to be out of a job soon?"

Max doesn't look any happier by the change of subject. "Artie's already taking charge. He's been talking with the board members, buttering everyone up. There's a board meeting to take the vote. Then I guess the sale will be a done deal."

He says it with such finality that something in me bristles. "Are you sure? From what I heard, the other board members don't even want to sell."

Max looks surprised. "I don't know. Artie can be pretty persuasive. And he's the one in charge, so—"

"That's the problem," I interrupt, remembering what Ernest told me. "They don't want to sell, but they need someone in charge who's going to lead the way. If you're just going to let Artie take over, they'll follow his lead."

"I don't really have a lot of choice," Max protests. "Artie *won*."

"He won the treasure hunt," I correct him, feeling a spark of rebellion. "The board still gets to vote on the sale. And the chairman, for that matter. So why aren't you in there fighting for it?"

"It's no use," Max says. "It's too late."

"No, it isn't!" I exclaim, getting angry now. "This isn't one of your assignments. You don't have to just stand on the sidelines observing, then leave when you've had enough. If you want that company, you've got to get in there and make it happen. Show them they've got an alternative. Unless . . ." I pause. "Unless all the things you said about being ready for the responsibility were just bullshit, and you're happy to get back to your life as an international playboy."

Max looks annoyed. "Is that really what you think of me?"

"Show me a reason not to," I counter.

There's a long pause. "You're right," he says. "Fuck. The meeting has probably started." He heads for the exit, then turns back to me. "Aren't you coming?"

I pause. Maybe I'm a glutton for punishment, but I need to see this through.

"OK. One last stop on this treasure hunt."

Before the game is really over.

25

HALLIE

I'VE NEVER BEEN SO impatient for an elevator in my life. And it's not even my company at stake. I tap my foot against the glossy floor in the Carlisle building's lobby as the numbers slowly creep down.

"Can we just take the stairs?" I ask.

"It's twenty floors up," Max replies.

"OK, maybe not."

Finally, the elevator door slides open and we pile inside.

"Thank you for coming with me for this," Max says quietly, catching my eye in the cramped space. "You were with me every step of the way before."

The words send a pang through my heart. "Yeah," I say. "I was."

Before he believed the worst in me, without even letting me explain.

He looks like he knows exactly what I'm thinking. "Look, I know maybe I can't take back what I did. I'll understand if you're really done with me after this. But just know I'm sorry, and that I want nothing but the best for you."

My heart aches, and I almost want to throw myself into those muscular arms. But then the elevator glides to a stop at the top floor, and there's no time for misguided making out. "This way." Max grabs my hand and pulls me down the hallway to a pair of double doors. He throws them open, revealing a massive boardroom—and a whole table full of people.

Who are now staring at us.

"What the hell are you doing?" Artie blusters, at the head of the table.

I gulp. It's like a Carlisle family reunion in here. Cordelia, Parker, and Brad are sitting beside Artie, looking peeved. There's a line of strangers, clearly confused, and on the other side of the table is Franklin Carlisle himself. His expression is unreadable, but his eyes gleam with curiosity.

Ernest Hammersmith catches my eye and gives a little wave. The eleven other figures just gape at us.

"Have you voted yet?" Max demands.

"You can't just barge in here like this," Artie splutters. "You don't have enough shares for voting rights. Get out."

"No," Max says firmly. He steps up to the table. "Did. You. Take. The. Vote?"

"We were just about to when you walked in," Ernest pipes up. "But I've got to say this is an interesting turn of events. Perhaps we should hear what the young man has to say before we do anything hasty."

A murmur of agreement passes around the table. Artie's face shifts from white to red. "Now look here—"

"Arthur Augustus Franklin Junior," Franklin says, in a voice that makes everyone fall silent. "Quiet."

Artie's mouth presses into a flat line. With a glare at Max, he sinks into his seat.

Max approaches the table. His face is determined, and there's a fierce light in his eyes that I've never seen before. Damn if it doesn't make him even hotter. But it's not his good looks that are going to convince the board not to take the easy way out.

"Carlisle Publishing has been around for nearly two hundred years," he begins, looking at each of the board members in turn. "That's a hell of a legacy. It's a heavy legacy, in some ways. I've spent a lot of my life trying to run away from it, chasing adventure instead of thinking about my responsibilities. Then three weeks ago my grandfather sent us on a scavenger hunt through the company's history. At first, I wasn't sure I was even going to stay in the running. But the farther I went, the more I realized how much this company matters. How much it matters to *me.*

"I learned a lot of things on that trip around the country. To recognize a good thing when it's right in front of me." He looks at me. "That great things come out of working as a team. And that there are people and places worth sticking around for and dedicating yourself to."

Oh boy. Seeing him like this, it's hard not melt into a puddle of sentimental goo. Despite all my best intentions, I can't deny it anymore: I'm in love with him.

Hopelessly, ridiculously in love.

Max looks around the table again. "Carlisle Publishing is one of those places. I don't want to lose the legacy we've built. I want to build it bigger, better, to meet the challenges ahead of us. I've seen how this business works from the ground level. I've been the one out there in the field, finding the stories that get printed and run around the world. I know I can take us even farther if you give me the chance."

He pauses. "So that's what I'm asking. For the chance to prove how much I care about this company. A chance to see how much we can build together." His gaze slides to me for just a second, and I can't help wondering if he's talking about more than just the business. "If I disappoint you, you can still sell in a year, or two, or whenever you feel it's time. But I don't think I will. I think we'll build something truly great together."

He steps back, and the room is silent. Even Artie looks stunned. He starts to open his mouth—but Ernest beats him to it.

"Hear, hear!" the gallery curator says. "Now that's more like it. I motion to install Max Carlisle as CEO and delay any sale offers pending the company's performance."

"Wait a minute!" Artie bursts out, but the murmurs rising around the table drown him out.

"Vote!" Ernest calls out. "All in favor of the motion?"

He holds up his hand. Other hands lift all around the table. All of them, in fact, except for Artie, Cordelia, Parker, and Brad. Even Franklin raises his hand. Artie shoots him a dirty look.

"You don't have any voting shares left."

His grandfather beams back at him. "I can still throw in my support."

"More than fifty percent in favor," Ernest announces. "The motion passes!"

He gets up out of his seat to shake Max's hand. If I thought Max had been lit up before, now he's absolutely glowing. The other board members crowd around. They only part when Franklin approaches.

"Max, my boy." Franklin sounds choked up. "Look at the man you've become. You kept me waiting long enough."

"Gramps." Max looks a little emotional, too. "I'm going to make you proud. I swear it."

"After today, I know you will," Franklin says. Then he leans in with a mischievous grin. "You know, this treasure hunt was only for my shares in the company. The rest of my estate is still up for grabs..."

There's a beat, and then Max laughs. "I'll be just fine," he says, slapping his grandfather's back.

"I know you will be, but one day you might be happy to be my heir. When you have a family of your own..." Franklin gives me a meaningful look, and Max tenses.

"I should go talk to the others," he says, and quickly walks away.

Watching the congratulations, a lump rises in my throat. This is

Max's moment. And I don't belong here. I'm not a Carlisle, and I never was. Our relationship was only just pretend.

I slip out of the room and hurry to the elevators. Funny how every time I'm heading down on one of these elegant cars, I find myself close to tears. But this time, I can't hold them back.

It's over.

And now I have to figure out what the future holds for me.

26

HALLIE

"HALLIE!" Jules exclaims the second I walk in the door. I stop in my tracks. She's not usually quite that enthusiastic to see me. You'd think I'd been missing for weeks. All I did was wander around Manhattan for a while, walking off some of my heartache, before I headed home.

"Jules," I reply slowly, looking her over for any signs that an alien being has taken over my roommate. No, she looks like her usual professional, collected self. Other than the slightly crazed gleam in her eyes.

"You haven't eaten yet, have you?" she says.

"Um, no."

"Perfect. We *have* to go grab some dinner." She grasps me by the elbow and hauls me right back out the door.

"Okay," I say, still bewildered. "Dinner sounds good, but what's the occasion? Did you win some major case or something?"

"No, no. I just thought— Your new job! We should celebrate your new job."

That would sound reasonable if I hadn't started that new job three days ago. And if we hadn't already gone for drinks. I eye her suspiciously as she ushers me down the hall. "Jules, are you feeling OK?"

"Sure. Just hungry!"

"I guess I could eat. I didn't get near craft service," I add. "And then . . ." Well, I'm not ready to talk about the whole Max part of my day.

Luckily, Jules seems distracted. She checks her phone as we head downstairs, then grabs my arm when I try to hail a cab. "We can walk!"

"In those heels?" I look down at her don't-fuck-with-me stilettos.

"They're comfortable. Really."

"Uh huh." I follow, suspicious, as she charges down the street. "Where do you want to eat?"

"This new place opened, right around the corner."

"Oh, great. What kind of food?"

"Mexican, or Greek, or something. How was your day?"

"Good. Melissa is letting me get more and more involved in the shoots." I pause, thinking about what happened *after* work. My heart squeezes. I don't think I want to bring that up right now. Jules has listened to me mope about Max for weeks. Whatever she's excited about, I don't want to ruin it by being a downer. "Anyway, all good there."

"That's awesome. I knew they were crazy not to take you on that first time around. Watch out, world! Hallie Gage, star photographer, has arrived."

I laugh. "I'm not quite there yet. But it does feel like I'm finally on my way."

Jules stops dead outside a nondescript building. "This is it."

I look up suspiciously. "Are you sure? It doesn't look like a restaurant."

"That's the gimmick," she says. "Like a pop-up, or secret, or whatever." She hits the buzzer, and then leads me inside a plain hallway.

"Real secret." I look around again. "Are you sure, because—"

Jules flings open a door at the end of the hallway, and I stop on the threshold,

"Jules?" I ask, slowly. "This isn't dinner."

It's a photography studio. The most stunning studio space I've ever seen. The windows are huge, with a whole wall of drop-cloth. There's a workbench already set with a dizzying array of cameras and equipment, at the far end lies a sleek black desk with a computer set up for editing, and there's even a space just off the main room, already set up as a dark room.

I look around in amazement. There isn't just a ton of equipment —it's top of the line. The lamps, the tripods . . . and the cameras . . . Fuck, there's that baby I've spent the last six months drooling over at the shop. Whoever runs this studio, they've got amazing taste.

Which begs the question . . . "Who owns this place?" I ask, turning to Jules. "What are we even doing here?"

Jules grins. "You do. It's yours."

"What?"

She hands me a note, smiling even wider.

HALLIE,

You know writing is my thing, not taking pictures, or I'd have been able to get this together a lot faster. But they tell me every piece of equipment in this place is the best you could possibly get. And you deserve the best. You wouldn't accept the money you earned, but I hope you'll accept this gift from me.

I'm also better at writing than talking, especially when something —or someone—matters to me this much. So in case I didn't make it clear before, doubting you is the worst decision I've ever made in my life. And believe me, I've made a lot of harebrained schemes in my time. You didn't just make me laugh and stand by me and turn me on more than any woman ever has. You've made me a better man. Being with you showed me how I want to be.

There's no way to put a price on that gift. This studio only

scratches the surface of repaying you, but it's the best I could think of. So take it. Follow your dreams. There's nothing that would make me happier than knowing I helped you reach them like you've helped me.

Everything's in your name. No strings attached. But if you're willing to take another chance on me, it'd make me even happier to be there with you. We only spent a week together, and already it's hard for me to imagine my life without you. I love you, Hallie. I'd do anything for the chance to show you how much, over and over, until you know you never have to doubt me again.

MAX

THE LETTER WAVERS in my hand. I read it again, blinking hard.

Oh my God.

"Hallie?" Jules asks from the doorway.

I stuff the letter into my purse and spin around. "Where is he?"

"I don't know. He dropped off the note this morning with instructions," she tells me.

Which means he'd planned this, all along. Even before he won the company back.

"I have to go!" I hug her quickly. "I might still be able to catch him."

I dash outside and flag a cab down. "The Carlisle Publishing building," I tell the driver. "Fast, please?"

"I can do fast." He hits the gas, and we race away.

It takes way too long to get over the bridge. I'm ready to jump out and go on foot by the time we make it. I shove the driver a handful of bills run for the doors.

My pulse thumps all the way up to the top floor. I'm practically hyperventilating when the elevator door slides open and—

My heart sinks. The lights in the boardroom are out. A man in a janitor's outfit is clearing away the empty coffee cups.

I pull out my cellphone and dial. *Pick up, pick up, pick up . . .*

"Hallie?" Max's voice says in my ear.

My heart leaps. "Max!"

He says something, but there's so much background noise, I can't hear him.

"Max? I can't hear you. Where are you?"

"Wait . . . I'll go . . . anyway."

I want to shout in frustration. I listen closer, trying to pick up his words, but there's just a loud hum of conversation. Then someone yells, "A dozen glazed, three crullers!" and I know exactly where he is.

"Stay right there," I tell him. "I'm coming to you."

I burst from the Carlisle building doors and sprint across the street to the donut shop where Olivia and I had our first conversation. Where I got sucked into this whole crazy situation. I probably look like a mad person when I fling open the door. But the only person whose opinion I care about is the guy just getting up from his table.

Max steps forward to meet me. His smile is still a little hesitant, as if he's not sure what I'm here for. Well, I can clear that up real quick.

I grab him by his shirt pull him into a kiss.

A hot, deep, "take me now, I'm yours forever" kind of kiss.

Max's arms come around me, drawing me even closer. The press of his lips is so sure and perfect it sends shivers racing through me. God, how did I go three weeks without kissing this man? The idea of giving it up seems impossible.

Finally, we come up for air. "I'm really hoping that wasn't just a 'Congratulations on becoming CEO' kiss," he says.

I laugh. "No. I guess you could say it was a 'Here's your second chance and you'd better not blow it' kiss." I take a breath. "And also, I love you too."

Max's expression changes, and he kisses me again, with a new possession in his touch.

"So you liked the studio?" he says when he releases me.

"Like it?" I laugh. "I'm pretty sure I'm in love with it, too. You're going to have some tough competition for my attention."

He chuckles. "I wouldn't have it any other way. Competition seems to bring out the best in us, don't you think?"

"Hmm, most of the time."

His gaze lowers for a second. "Your roommate chewed me out twice as good as I've already done to myself. But if you need some more apologizing . . ."

"No," I stop him. "That's okay." I touch his cheek. "I'm convinced. The studio is amazing. That goes without saying. But really it was the letter that sold me."

Max bends his head close to mine. "I have been told I have a way with words. There are plenty more where those came from."

I laugh, a little breathless. "Do go on. I'm looking forward to hearing all of them. On one condition."

"Anything."

"That we're naked in bed," I grin. "With a box of those glazed donuts, to go."

HALLIE

"OKAY, lean a little more into the light. There, that's it. Show off that handsome face!"

Jack laughs, and I snap a photo of that expression too. "I'm going on the cover of a business magazine, not *GQ*," he reminds me.

"Yeah, well, you want the ladies picking up that magazine too, don't you?" I grin at my former boss and then glance across the studio —*my* studio—to his girlfriend. "You don't mind, do you, McKenna?"

She grins back. "He might as well cash in on those good looks while he still has them."

"*Hey!*" Jack protests. "Where do you think they're going?"

"Well, maybe you'll find some eternal youth potion to invest in. But don't worry—if you don't, I'll still love you when you're old and wrinkly."

"That's a relief," Jack mutters, but he can't hide his smile. Hard to imagine he's the guy who used to have a revolving door of women coming in and out of his life, but McKenna has brought out his mush-ball side. Probably to the benefit of whatever executive assistant replaced me at his office.

"Off the stool now," I say, motioning at him. "Let's get some standing shots. Give me a pose like you just made a billion dollars off an investment and it's not even that big a deal to you."

Jack snorts, but he strikes the perfect pose anyway. I give him a thumbs up and start snapping.

Times like this, I feel like pinching myself to make sure this is really my life and not a literal dream. Carlisle Publishing let me transition from photo assistant to close-to-fulltime photographer with a little help from Melissa, and now I only head out onto sets with her a couple times a week. Which is actually great, because she's still teaching me tons.

Plus, for the first time ever, I've been able to do *Jack* a business-related favor. Max decided to revamp the company's main business mag, and I pitched my former boss as the cover story for the first issue. So naturally I got dibs on the photo shoot.

We break so Jack can take a drink and stretch his legs. My phone pings with an incoming text. It's from Max.

Hey, sweetheart, how late are you working? I need my Hallie fix.

I smile. *Probably no more than another hour. You want me to come over after?*

I'll make it worth your while. He adds in a kissing emoji. *And I've got a surprise for you.*

Oooh, what did you do?

If I told you, it wouldn't be a surprise, would it? Just get your cute ass over here and you'll find out.

Tease, I shoot back.

Oh, I can tease even better than that if I wanted to. He signs off with a wink.

"The boyfriend?" McKenna asks when she sees my expression.

"Yeah." My smile is probably giddy, but who cares? It's hard to hold back how happy I am.

We wrap up the shoot in just half an hour. Jack stops on his way out to give my shoulder a quick squeeze. "It's great to see you doing so well, Hallie," he says. "Looks like quitting working for me was the best thing that ever happened to you."

"Oh, I don't regret that time," I say. "I learned an awful lot. Particularly about keeping guys like you in line."

He laughs. "Say hi to Max for me."

I hop in a cab to Max's apartment, on the top floor of a brownstone that somehow puts even Olivia's Agency building to shame. When I reach the apartment door, I come to a sudden halt.

There's an envelope taped to it. A way-too-familiar-looking linen envelope. My guy does have a sense of humor.

I grab it and rip it open. Surprise, surprise, there's a slip of paper inside with a clue on it. Although Max's style is a little different from his grandfather's.

I drank it first with you
Come in and let's have round two

Oh-kay. A drink. In the kitchen seems like a fair guess. The door's unlocked, so I slip inside and head into that room of shining stainless steel and marble.

A bottle of cognac and a snifter are sitting on the counter. Even though it's been a couple of months, I recognize the label. It's the same stuff Max ordered when we met to discuss the job posing as his girlfriend. How could I forget? It was damn good stuff.

I pour some into the glass and take a sip. Yep, still fucking amazing. I'm liking this treasure hunt a hell of a lot more than Franklin's version already.

Another linen envelope was resting under the bottle. Another clue.

Lots of books up on the shelves
We'll write our story for ourselves

The bookshelves are in the living room. I carry the cognac glass over. A red rose is lying on one of the shelves on top of a third envelope. I pick it up and sniff the sweet scent. I have no idea what got into Max, but I'm definitely not complaining. My pulse thumps a little faster in anticipation as I open the next clue.

On silky sheets we rest or play
Now it's time to hear what I have to say

I laugh a little to myself, making my way around the sofa and around the corner into the master bedroom.

My pulse skips when I see what's waiting for me. Candles are all across the dresser and the night tables. Max is sitting on the edge of the bed waiting for me, a grin on his face and a matching glass in his hand. He gets up and clinks it against mine.

"Glad you could make it."

"This is definitely a hunt I can get behind." I take another sip of the cognac. "What's the special occasion? I know you didn't get a promotion, because there's no higher position to promote you to."

He chuckles. "Always so impatient."

I set my hand on my hip. "You know I am. Is this all you have to say? Because after this build-up, I was expecting something a little more—"

Max sinks down onto one knee, pulling a box from his pocket.

Holy shit. My heart stops. All I can do is gape at him as he pops the box open. The diamond on the ring inside sparkles so bright it nearly blinds me. Or maybe that's just the tears springing into my eyes.

"Hallie Gage," he says, "I spent way too long not knowing I needed someone like you in my life. Now that I've found you, I want to make it forever. I want you by my side through the good times and the bad, wherever life takes us. What do you say to the crazy, epic adventure of marrying me?"

I'm so choked up it takes me a moment to find words. A breathless giggle spills out of me. "Yes. Yes, of course I will!"

I grab the front of his shirt to tug him up. He pulls me into his arms, and I'm already pressing my mouth to his. I kiss him hard, with all the joy that's swelling inside me. Crazy—maybe. Epic—for sure. I wouldn't miss this adventure for the world.

Max kisses me back deeply, until all that joy starts to turn into desire. I run my fingers into his hair as our tongues tease over each other. He tips my head to kiss me even more thoroughly. A hot bolt of lust shoots through me.

Before I can act on it, Max eases back. His eyes are bright with a matching desire. He holds up the box. "I think we'd better get this ring on you before we forget all about it."

"Not much chance of that." I hold up my hand, a giddy shiver racing through me. Max slides the ring over my finger. I set my hand against his chest, admiring the sparkle.

"Is it OK?" he asks.

I grin. "It's even more beautiful than the fake one."

"Oh, there was nothing fake about that ring."

"You know what I mean." I laugh imagining decades and decades with this spectacular man. Then I curl my fingers into his shirt again and yank his mouth back to mine.

We tumble over onto the bed. I think I dropped my cognac some-where back there, but I don't really give a fuck, not with Max kissing my neck as I fumble with the buttons on his shirt. His tongue slides over the sensitive skin at the base of my throat, and I gasp. We strip off each other's clothes, and I press up against him with a needy whimper. He groans, teasing his thumb over one nipple and then claiming it with his mouth. Another moan slips out of me.

As he has his way with my other breast, his hand dips under my panties. I arch into his touch with a gasp. He traces his fingers around my clit with a gentle precision that leaves me shaking.

"More," I gasp, and then he's pushing me back on the sheets, moving down my body.

His tongue slicks over my clit, and a bolt of pleasure sizzles through me. But as good as I know he can give, I want him closer than this. I want to feel him all. I want him inside me, as deep as he can go.

"Max," I plead, pulling at his shoulders. He doesn't argue. He braces himself over me, and we lose ourselves in another searing kiss. His body rocks against me, his cock grazing my core. My fingernails dig into his back, and he slides deep inside. I moan, gripping him with my thighs. He gazes into my eyes as he fills me completely, lust and adoration mingling in his gaze. I touch his cheek, drawing his face down to mine.

"I love you," I say against his lips.

He kisses me hard. "I love you too. And, fuck, I love how you feel, too."

"Mmm." That's all I can manage to say as he starts to move inside me. He seems to fill me more with each thrust. Pleasure radiates through me. I rock to meet him, and we find our rhythm together.

Max groans, burying his head against my shoulder. He grasps my thighs and angles even deeper. I shudder against him with a rush of bliss. "Oh, God. Right there. Fuck."

He starts to chuckle, but it's lost in another groan. His thrusts speed up, hitting just the right spot, and my orgasm explodes through me. I gasp, clutching him. Max makes a choked sound, right there with me.

When I surface, I'm panting and boneless and utterly sated. Not that I can imagine ever having enough of this man. He stays over me, kissing my cheek, smiling when I meet his eyes.

"Was that an enthusiastic enough yes for you?" I ask, fluttering my eyelashes.

He laughs and rolls over, gathering me against him. "Here's to many, many more."

Our adventure has only just begun.

EPILOGUE

CAL

AS A RULE, I try to stay away from engagement parties. Weddings, too. Baby showers, anniversary shin-digs – basically, any event where the women get that special gleam in their eyes. The one that says, '*Commitment*', as if they're already planning the side-by-side rockers on the front porch somewhere and all they need's the right sucker—I mean, partner, to rock into an early grave with them.

But sometimes, duty calls. Like tonight, celebrating my buddy Max popping the question to his girlfriend, Hallie.

"For an engagement party, this isn't terrible," I admit, glancing around the room. Max booked out one of his favorite restaurants for the night, and it's packed with familiar faces. "Although, I remember the days when a night out with you meant waking up in Buenos Aires with no passport and the women's beach volleyball team. Good times."

Max laughs. "I'm a changed man, my friend. True love will do that to you."

"I'll take your word for it."

I grab a drink, pleased at least that domestic bliss hasn't changed the man's taste in scotch.

"What about you?" Max asks. "Things have been so crazy with Hallie, I haven't seen you in forever."

I take a reluctant breath. "Things are... complicated." I reply.

"Trouble at the company?" Max looks surprised. "I thought McAdams was having a stellar year. Remind me to get on the waiting list for the new model," he adds. "I hear that beauty runs like a dream."

"She does," I nod. For once, business is the least of my concerns. The auto company that bears my family's name has been out-performing across the board, especially our luxury car division – my personal baby. Our new energy-efficient models have waiting lists over a year long, and rival Tesla as the new status car of choice among CEOs and A-list celebrities. "No, this is personal."

"Oh really?" Max smirks. "What's her name?"

I give a hollow laugh. "I wish it were that simple." I pause, suddenly realizing that Max might have the answer to my problem, after all. "How did this all work?" I ask. "I mean, hiring Hallie to play your girlfriend."

Max hushes me, and I remember, they're keeping their uncon-ventional meeting under wraps. "Sorry," I say quickly.

"That's OK." Max studies me. "Don't tell me you need to put on a show? I thought jet-setting playboy was the McAdams brand."

"Things change," I say, not wanting to get into the details right now. "Let's just say, I have my reasons."

Two of them, to be exact. Aged ten and eight, a handful at the best of times, but now is most definitely not that time.

"Talk to Olivia," Max tells me. "Over in the corner, the blonde."

He points to a cool, elegant woman across the room. "Thanks."

"But watch out." Max grins. "These arrangements have a way of getting out of hand."

"Not for me," I reply grimly, and strike out across the room. I'm not off on some wild treasure hunt like Max was. No, for me, the stakes are much higher than that.

I have three days to find a wife, and the clock is ticking.

TO BE CONTINUED...
Cal's story is just getting started! The next Billionaire Bachelor book
HOT DADDY is coming soon -
Order now!

Hot Daddy
Billionaire Bachelors: Book 2

WELCOME to the Billionaire Bachelors series, where the sexiest men in the city are about to meet their match...

Playboy CEO, Cal McAdams, lives life in the fast lane: hot women, hotter deals, and... a fake fiancee? I signed on to help reform his reckless image and win custody of his god-children, but I wasn't expecting to come face-to-face (and mouth-to-mouth) with my wild Vegas hook-up from three years ago.

AKA, 6"3 of tanned muscle, sharp suits, and 'undress me' eyes.

AAKA, the best thigh-clenching, bed-shaking sex of my life.

AAAKA, the man who couldn't be more off-limits if he had a uranium belt wrapped around his, um, assets.

I've never been one to break the rules, but Cal has me wanting to rip them up - and roll around naked on the scrap paper. But with just three weeks to turn this bachelor into a DILF, can we keep our crazy chemistry from derailing his plans? Or will gold-digging relatives, rambunctious pre-teens, and a little thing called love leave us both crashed out of the race?

Find out in the new sexy, hilarious romantic comedy from Lila Monroe!

Have you discovered my Lucky in Love series? These sexy romantic comedies all feature alpha men, sassy heroines - and laugh-out-loud shenanigans.

BOOK #1:

GET LUCKY

What happens when you wake up in a hotel suite next to a gorgeous naked man with absolutely no memory of the past twelve hours?

I guess it's true what they say. What happens in Vegas stays in Vegas.

Or at least I hope it stays here. The Romantic Style convention was meant to be a weekend of raucous fun with friends, sun, and enough poolside margaritas to forget about my ex. But now, instead of meeting my fans and signing books, I'm stuck with cocky divorce lawyer Nate Wexler. He's arrogant, infuriating, and I can't keep my hands off of him. Judging by the state of our hotel room, last night was wild. I just wish I could remember it.

A pair of matching tattoos. A cheap wedding veil. A half empty box of glow in the dark condoms.

What the hell just happened?

Discover the hot and hilarious world of the LUCKY IN LOVE series from Lila Monroe!

Available now!

The Billionaire Bargain Series

Sexy Australian billionaire Grant Devlin is ruining my life. He exercises shirtless in his office, is notorious for his lunchtime hook-ups, he even yawns sexily. If I didn't need this job so bad, I'd take his black Amex and tell him where to swipe it.

He doesn't even know I exist, but why would he? He jets off to Paris with supermodels, I spend Friday nights with Netflix and a chunk of Pepperidge Farm frozen cake--waiting for his call. Because every time he crashes his yacht, or blows $500k on a single roulette spin in Monte Carlo, I'm the PR girl who has to clean up his mess.

But this time, it's going to take more than just a fat charity donation. This time, the whole company is on the line. He needs to show investors that he's settling down, and Step #1 is pretending to date a nice, stable girl until people forget about what happened with the Playboy Bunnies backstage at the Oscars.

My plan is perfect, except for one thing: He picks me.

Available Now!

ABOUT THE AUTHOR

Combining her love of writing, sex and well-fitted suits, Lila Monroe wrote her first serial, The Billionaire Bargain, in 2015. She weaves sex, humor and romance into tales about hard-headed men and the strong and sassy women who try to tame... love... tame them.

***

www.lilemonroebooks.com
lila@lilamonroebooks.com

ALSO BY LILA:

Made in the USA
Columbia, SC
30 August 2019